D1191079

TODAY I AM A HAM

Other Books by Ethelyn M. Parkinson

THE OPERATION
    THAT HAPPENED TO RUPERT PIPER

THE TERRIBLE TROUBLES
    OF RUPERT PIPER

THE MERRY MAD BACHELORS

GOOD OLD ARCHIBALD

TODAY I AM A HAM

Ethelyn M. Parkinson

illustrations by Ralph J. McDonald

ABINGDON PRESS

Nashville / New York

Standard Book Number: 687-42190-X

COPYRIGHT © 1968 by Abingdon Press
All Rights Reserved
Printed in the U.S.A.
Library of Congress Catalog Card Number 68:10705

P248

ROANOKE BIBLE COLLEGE LIBRARY
ELIZABETH CITY, N. C.

With love to

Catherine

who knows that there's absolutely nothing
like having a ham in the house—unless it's
having two!

19,952

Contents

The Coach's Son Flops

Of course, I knew it was coming. Every time I tackled the wrong man or couldn't hang onto the ball when it was socked right into my arms, every time I tripped over myself, every time I goofed up a play, I expected to hear Coach Durbin howl, "You, there! Eric Crane! Over here!"

Then I would get the bad news. I had dreamed three times just how it would look in the *West Comet Clarion.*

ANDY'S SON FLOPS!
Andrew Crane, West Comet Senior High's tragic athletic coach, got out his crying towel with real reason today. Over in the practice field behind the Junior High Halls of Learning, Coach Peter Durbin sifted his flock of seventh-grade hopefuls and turned thumbs down on—you guessed it!—young Eric, the Crane son and heir. . . .

About there I would wake up in a sweat, wishing things. Wishing I had muscles, like Harve Bonner, who was only a junior, but was captain of Dad's Senior High football team. Or wishing that, besides my three sisters, Dad had three or four other sons, all athletes. Or wishing another impossible one—that I was Charlie Korth.

Don't picture Charlie with muscles. He's like me, all legs and arms and skin and bones. He looks better, though, because his hair is black and straight and his eyes are black and snappy. I've got reddish hair that curls up, if it gets long enough, and some freckles, but not enough to make me look rugged, and eyes that are a kind of worried blue. I usually look desperate, and I've got reasons.

No, I don't look like Charlie, but that wasn't the main reason I wished, sometimes, that I was he. The thing was, Charlie's dad didn't give a hoot whether Charlie made the team or not!

Besides, Charlie was learning to be a radio ham.

Well, after my third nightmare I told Charlie, "The real thing won't be worse than my dreams."

We were hustling to school. Charlie shrugged. "You take it too hard, Eric. I know I'll get kicked out, too, but I'm not losing any sleep!"

"Your dad won't care. He wants you to take over his drugstore some day. Your family won't be disgraced."

"Family?" Charlie stared. "Jill won't be disgraced!"

Jill is my third sister. Real neat. My parents got us both the same year. I was the New Year baby. You know, the first citizen born in town that year. The stores gave me darling little blue things. And because Dad already had Frances and Kristan, his friends were delighted. "Andy Crane has a brand new quarterback, all his own!" That sort of thing.

Mother saved the clippings.

Well, the next December, that same year, Jill came

along. And am I glad she did! I don't know what I'd *do* without Jill!

"No," I said, "Jill knows a guy can't help it if he isn't a born football player. But Frances—well, you know the Princess!"

Francie looks like a princess, with blonde hair and big blue eyes and a sweet little mouth—when she's not yelling—and she sure gives us the princess treatment!

"Yeah!" Charlie said. "Francie thinks the whole world ought to be like Harve Bonner—musclebound!"

My sister Kristan, with some girls, passed us about then. Charlie winked at me and talked louder. "After scrimmage tonight, come over to my shack."

Sure enough, Kristan looked back, horrified. Kris isn't the Princess, although some fellows think she is cuter. Her eyes are blue, too. Her hair is brown and kind of long and shiny. She has a real straight little nose and very white teeth, and she seems brisk, like, clean, fresh air. Kris is very sanitary. She is a high honor student, and there are quite a few things that bug her. Charlie knew them all.

"Charlie Korth," she said, "what a shocking term to use for your home!"

"My shack ain't my home," Charlie said—but softly. Not even Charlie Korth says "ain't" in Kristan Crane's presence. We snickered.

"Charlie," I said, "I bet today is the last day I'll go to your shack from scrimmage. I may go from history class, or home, or Chicago or Patagonia, but not from scrimmage. I have a feeling this is *the* day!"

Scrimmage went as usual. Coach Durbin yelled,

"You, there! That the way you run interference?" And, "You, there! That how you tackle?" And, "For Pete's sake, man, pick yourself up and get going!"

Some girls came along to watch. I could see Jill, with Betsy Burnside. Betsy lives next door to us and is quite keen, when you consider what she has to buck. She has Mrs. Mattie Burnside for a mother, and that creep Webber Burnside for a brother. It is not easy.

The girls were watching when I socked into my own quarterback as he tried a sneak. I landed in a heap.

"Crane!" Coach Durbin yelled. "Over here!"

Charlie helped me up. "Eric," he said, "your dreams are coming true!"

I moaned.

Charlie was right. The only thing was, Coach prolonged the agony. "Eric—" He put a big hand on my shoulder. I felt as if he was forcing me right into the ground. "You know, Eric, to be a football player there are a few things a fellow ought to have."

I knew that, and I knew I didn't have them.

"You need backbone," Coach Durbin said. "Drive. Power. Muscle. And—shall we say—aptitude! Now, a-hem! You should inherit these things. You'll change lots in oh, say, another year. But—a-hem!"

Jill and Betsy were standing a little way off, looking as if this was my funeral. Coach put his arm around Charlie, and I guessed he was going to make him captain.

He said, "Eric, why don't you and Charlie just forget about football this fall? Turn in some good grades, and see what a year does to you!"

12

"A *year!*" I moaned, when we walked toward home. "Charlie, I can't go home! I can't tell Dad!"

Jill and Betsy were waiting down the street. They're always together.

Like my other sisters, Jill has blue eyes. She has light brown hair that comes down straight to her shoulders and then curls up, and she has straight bangs.

Betsy has reddish, curly hair and a little turned-up nose with a few freckles on it. Her eyes are blue, too, but her eyelashes are kind of reddish gold and curly, like her hair. They always say she looks more like me than Jill does.

"It's a gyp, Eric!" Betsy was almost crying. "You didn't fall hard! I mean, you fell—better than last scrimmage!"

"That's so!" Jill was almost crying, too. "That last fall was—well, not half so flat—or sprawly—as yesterday!"

"Thanks," I said. "Thanks, anyway."

"Eric?" Betsy's face was pink. "Eric, shall I get Coach Durbin fired? I've got connections, you know."

Mr. Burnside is the banker in West Comet. Also, he's on the school board.

"Thanks, but forget it!" I said. "Jeeps, I wouldn't want Dad fired every time he kicks a kid off a team!"

"The problem is," Charlie said, "who's going to tell your dad?"

"I'll tell him," Jill said. "I'll just begin, 'Daddy—'"

"'Daddy, brace yourself!'" Charlie suggested.

Jill gasped. "Charlie Korth, I *hope* I'll use more tact than that!"

Charlie kicked the walk. It sure bothers him when Jill doesn't like his ideas.

Betsy tried. "'Dad, I am very happy to tell you that—'"

"*Happy!*" I almost choked. "Get *with* it!"

Betsy blushed. I was sorry. Betsy *is* the best Burnside.

"That's OK," I said. "You *tried.*"

Jill tried again, "'Daddy, I know how you've always felt about decisions. About making decisions and sticking to them. I've always admired—our whole family—Mother, Francie, Kristan—the entire family has always admired the way *you* make decisions, and—"

"*Jill!*" I was sweating. "You'll have to come to the point sometime! And the point is that Coach Durbin gave me the bounce!"

We stood there thinking about it. "Is the market high or low at your house?" Charlie asked me anxiously.

"Depends on Dad's scrimmage this afternoon," I said.

Everyone knows the market's low around our house if Dad's scrimmage is bad or if a tough game is coming up. If he loses a game, it's *dirge.*

"Look, Jill," I said. "I'm going over to Charlie's shack. You'll tell Dad?"

She nodded and tried to smile.

Charlie and I went on toward his place, walking faster and faster. We could hardly wait to get to Charlie's shack. Sometimes I thought the only thing I wanted in the world was to be a ham operator and have a radio shack like Charlie's.

But the truth was, I wanted something else even

14

more. I wanted my dad to think I was a success, not a flop. And I didn't see a chance!

Mr. Korth had come home from his drugstore to take Mrs. Korth shopping. They had been having coffee in the kitchen and now she was putting her grocery list in her purse and Mr. Korth was jingling his keys.

He smiled at us. "Scrimmage over?"

"Over forever, Pa!" Charlie said. "Coach Durbin feels he can make it without me."

"No!" Mr. Korth laughed and looked like Charlie. "I'm desolated! Aren't you, Mother?"

Charlie's mother is real plump and real keen. She said, "Well, *we* like you, Charlie! Don't you let it get you down!"

"Not a bit of it!" Mr. Korth said. "There are other things in life besides football!"

I sighed. I would give anything in the world to hear my father say those words!

"You'll have to carry on, Eric," Mrs. Korth told me.

My face burned. "Well," I said, "well, Mrs. Korth, I won't be carrying on."

"Oh, *man!*" Mr. Korth whistled. "Don't *tell* me!" He kind of hugged me. "That dad of yours—"

"It will hit him hard," I said. "Frances, too, on account she wants Harve Bonner to think her family is good enough for him. Kris will suggest I make up for it some painful way, like hitting the books harder. And Ma—"

"Your mother will be perfectly satisfied," Mrs. Korth said. "And so am I. Football is not everything. Now, you two just have some cookies, and don't you worry!"

15

We took the cookies up to the shack. Up to heaven.

Did Charlie love his shack! I loved it, too, and I hadn't been there for a week.

A ham has to have a room for his equipment, where he can have privacy at all hours. That's his shack, and it's a very sacred place, to a ham.

Charlie wasn't really a ham, yet. He was just getting started. His shack was a little bit of a bedroom at the back of the Korths' upstairs. It was next to Charlie's own bedroom, and his dad was going to promise any day, now, to make a door between Charlie's room and his shack.

"Even if it's a little dog door," Charlie said. "Boy, it will be keen!"

"Pretty nice," I said. "Especially after you get kicked off the team!"

Charlie had a new sign on the door of his shack. KEEP OUT!

"That's for creeps," he said. "And jerks. Come on in!"

We went into the shack and he turned on the light, although it was still light outside. Charlie had his shack really furnished. He had a table with his short wave receiver and code practice set and stuff on it. There was a little red rag rug on the floor, and there were two chairs.

He let me have the red chair, and he took the funny one. We looked around. "Sometimes," Charlie said, "I just sit here and picture these walls all papered with QSL cards!"

"QSL cards?"

"You get them from hams to verify contacts. Of course, you send them, too. Mr. Kirby has them from all over the world, mostly."

I could picture them, too.

Charlie dragged his code practice set up close. "Here!" He propped up his code chart. "I'm learning code from this. I'm still on Group I." It meant he could send E, I, S, H, and 5.

"However," he said, "I've added T, M, O, and A. Mr. Kirby said to work on that much for a while. But you just use the code chart to check. I mean, you learn by listening. By sound. Will you copy? Here's a pencil."

He began to send, pounding out letters in code. I copied on his notebook, checking his dits and dahs with the chart, when I had to. He did the letters over and over. He mixed them up, various ways.

Suddenly I yelled, "Hey! You *said* something! You said, 'He is Amos'!"

Was Charlie ever happy, because I got it! "Copy this!" He began to pound.

"It took you forever," I told him after a while, "but I got, 'He is a hot shot.'"

"Great!" Charlie laughed. "Great, old man!"

My heart jumped. That's what hams sometimes call each other on the air. Old man. "Charlie," I said, "I've got to be a ham! Do you think Mr. Kirby would teach me?"

"I could name twenty guys he has taught. More than twenty!"

"What does he charge?"

"Nothing. Hams help each other."

18

"But this stuff! The code practice set! The receiver!"

"Well—" Charlie looked worried. "I got the code practice set for fifteen dollars. But you can always make one."

"I've got six dollars, and I'm supposed to get my bicycle repaired. But I don't want to wait," I said. "I want to learn with you. I'm telling Dad I need nine dollars!"

We looked at each other, both thinking that, under the terrible circumstances, chances were slim.

Mrs. Korth called up the stairs. "Dinner's ready! Eric, we'd love to have you stay!"

It was half past six, and I almost died. "I didn't know it was that late! I'd better run!"

When I'm late I'm to blame for everything, so I *meant* run!

When I got home I could smell dinner, and trouble. Dad was late, too, so Jill hadn't had a chance to tell him about Coach Durbin and me. Francie was on the phone with Dot Speaker. Usually she's in her blue shirttail, but this night she was dressed up and smelled perfumey.

She hung up and pitched into me. "Eric Crane, exactly what do you mean by coming home at seven o'clock?"

"It's 6:35," I said. I can run home from Charlie's in three minutes.

"By my watch, it's seven!" Francie said. "And you *know* my date with Harve is at half past! Because you *know* Daddy won't let Harve stay out after nine!"

Kristan came downstairs all glowing from a good hot

bath and a heartwarming session with her geometry assignment. She sniffed.

"Eric Crane, you smell unsanitary! Where have you been?"

Well, I hadn't been in scrimmage long enough to need a shower. But Mrs. Burnside was in the kitchen with Mom, and I knew she was listening in. So I just said, "I had a very difficult after school."

"A very difficult what?"

But I was on my way upstairs.

It just bugs Kris if you leave a word out of something you say. While she's figuring on it, you can get out of her sight.

As I climbed, I heard Mrs. Burnside telling Ma, "I suppose I should be thankful, Hilda! Webber always comes straight home to his beloved violin. John Spencer says Webber keeps him constantly amazed—"

I knew! Webber didn't get much outdoor exercise, so he practiced with his window open. I knew all about it!

I hurried to get a shower. Combing my hair, I noticed I looked more desperate than ever. "Jeeps!" I said to myself. "After what happened, you'd like to ask Pa for nine dollars! Man, what colossal optimism and courage! I sure wish you *had* it!"

When I went downstairs, Dad had come and I knew the market was low. The girls were tiptoeing. "Scrimmage was bad!" Jill hissed. "Daddy says Almeda will beat us Saturday!"

I moaned. "Oh, boy, when scrimmage goes bad I wish I was a hundred miles away!"

"When scrimmage goes *badly*," Kris said. "And it's, 'I wish I *were* one hundred miles away.'"

"You're wrong, Kris," I said. "Make it one thousand!"

Ma was working over the Swiss steak. She had on her pink dress. I think Kris looks the most like Mom, but not one of my sisters looks just like her. Ma's hair is dark, like her eyes. She's not big and not too small. Just right. She's almost always smiling, and she's pretty. She's tops. Being a coach's wife is not easy.

Dinner was something. Dad didn't even know it was Swiss steak. You could tell he was picturing that team, thinking about plays, thinking about players. I watched him and wished I looked like him.

He's got red hair, too, but his looks crisp. He wears a butch. He's got sharp blue eyes and a hard, tough jaw. Some football players are bigger than he is, but Andy Crane is tough. And no matter what you might think sometimes, he's one wonderful guy. His teams know that.

Suddenly he looked me over. "You been out in the air, Skipper?"

Well, I ran home from Charlie's. "Yeah. I was," I said.

He nodded. He was thinking about scrimmage again. "That lunk of a Williamson! I can't get it through his head that when his job's to run interference, he's to run, and that there's no point in steaming off toward the goal headlong, unless he's got the ball!—*Francie!*"

Francie was peeking at her watch. She jumped. "Yes, Daddy?"

"You're all horsed up. If you've got a date with that clod of a Bonner tonight, you see that he's home at nine!"

"Daddy!" Francie wailed. "It's after seven, now!"

"You heard me! Nine o'clock, or I'll bench him!"

"Daddy, Harve's been playing good, hasn't he?"

"Playing well," Kristan said, under her breath.

"Neither!" Pa yelled. "Neither good nor well! I want that conference championship this year!"

The telephone rang. Frances and Jill sprang up.

"Maybe it's Harve!"

"Maybe it's Betsy!"

"Sit down," Mom said. "I'll get it. It's Mattie Burnside. She's worried because I'm behind with my painting."

Ma belongs to the Ingeborg Bloomer Music and Art Colony.

She said, "Hello, Mattie? Oh! Yes, Andy's here! Just a moment, Peter!"

Peter. Coach Durbin, over at Junior High. I turned cold.

We heard Dad. "Oh, so-so, Pete. . . . Sometimes I wonder if I'll get a team out of it. . . . Right! If we can just edge Almeda, Saturday. . . . If you lose the first game, it's a jinx. . . . What have you got this year? Anything good coming up?"

A long, terrible silence, while I felt the world coming to a painful end. At last the phone clicked. Pa came back to the table sagging all over. Ma put a piece of pumpkin pie in front of him and a cup of boiling coffee. He took up his fork.

22

Then he looked at me. "Well, Skipper?" His voice was terribly gentle. "So you—didn't make it."

I choked. "Dad, I—I tried."

I wished to heaven someone would say, "Football isn't everything!" But nobody said it, because in our house football *was* everything.

Jill was trying to keep from bawling. Francie was looking stunned, wondering what Harve would think.

"Eric," Kris said, "if you can't be an athlete, maybe you can be something else. Like—Webber Burnside, with his violin!"

"Webber Burnside!" Dad yelled. "Girl, have you *no* ambition?"

Right there Ma broke up and laughed.

Dad peeked at her out of the side of his eyes. He sure thinks she's pretty. You can tell. But he's just baffled if she laughs when things seem dead serious.

Mom wiped her eyes. "Eric, eat another piece of pie, dear. You'll grow a lot this year." She patted Kris. "Webber's sweet, honey, but Eric doesn't have to be like him."

Well, I was glad of that, but it was no time to ask for nine dollars. And it was the first time I ever ate a second piece of pumpkin pie without tasting it.

Mean John's Great Kindness

The next morning Charlie Korth was waiting at the corner. One look at me told all. "No nine dollars!"

"Coach Durbin broke the bad news to Pa," I said. "Jeeps, Charlie, I don't know why a guy like Dad had to have a son who's a flop!"

"You're no flop, Eric!"

"Count 'em on this one hand!" I stuck my hand in front of Charlie's face. "Count the people who like me! Jill and Ma! A very short list!"

"There's Betsy. And Mrs. Burnside hasn't given up hope. She keeps on trying to reform you."

"I mean at home. Kris and Francie are off the list. Kris thinks I'm why Webber Burnside doesn't come over. And the Princess had a big fight with Harve. He said she was late for the date and she said it was because I was late for dinner."

"Your dad was late, too."

"I'm always to blame," I said.

Charlie's black eyes crinkled. He laughed. "Know what, Eric? If you're ever a coach, you'll be more tragic than your dad, with a bigger, wetter crying towel!"

"You're a big help," I said. "How am I going to be a ham on six bucks, that's supposed to go into my bike? I wish it would snow!"

Charlie stared. "Snow? In September?"

"So I could shovel snow for extra money."

Charlie had news for me that night, up in his shack. "Eric, what you need most is a receiver. Bill Adkins knows where there's an old radio with a shortwave band that a guy will sell for five dollars. Lots of fellows start with a radio like that. And you can make your code practice set. You can buy the parts down at Mean John's."

"Way back there where you mentioned five bucks the deal fell through," I said.

"Look, Eric. Tell your dad hams have saved lives. Tell him they help out in emergencies." Charlie pulled the code practice set over. "Tell him if you can't be a ham you want a violin."

We both snickered.

Charlie sent several sentences: "She is his sis." "Mattie is his mom."

"You're getting good," I said.

"So are you."

"Me?"

"You're copying, aren't you? And you hardly looked at the chart. Here! Try sending."

I tried. "It isn't easy as it looks," I said.

"You should hear Mr. Kirby send," Charlie said. "Boy, has he ever got a good fist! He thinks I'm going to have one, too."

We took turns, sending and copying. It got late again.

"I'll get blasted," I said, "but I don't care. Charlie, if the market's up or down, my dad is going to be told I need ten bucks—for the radio and for parts for the code practice set. I'll pay him back when it snows."

25

When I got home Betsy and Jill were in the front hall. Betsy had probably been just leaving for half an hour.

"Dad home?" I asked.

"Not yet."

"Listen, Jill. I've *got* to have ten dollars so I can be a ham. Could you tell him?"

"My allowance is tomorrow, Eric!" Betsy said. "And, honestly, I can't think of a thing I want! I don't know what to do with so much money!"

"Two-fifty," I said. "You'll think of something. Besides, your mother would feel I'm a very bad investment. Jill, you ask Dad. Tell him hams are unsung heroes. The—the white hope of the country!"

"Sure. I'll tell him. But Eric, I've got three dollars—"

"You think Dad won't come through!"

She shook her head. "The market's low. Daddy threatened to kick Harve Bonner off the team!"

"Harve?" I choked. "His best player? There's some mistake!"

"You *think* so! Look at Francie!"

Francie was on the sofa on her stomach with her face in a pillow. "She dead?" I said. "Did she go and die, in all those rollers that nobody knows how to get out of her hair?"

"No," Ma said. "She just moved a little." Ma had her easel set up in a corner of the living room, and she was working on her painting. "I think Francie's posing for me. Still life. *Aren't* you, dear?"

Frances reared up and glared. *"Mo*-ther! Must you indulge that weird sense of humor at a time like this?"

Her voice shook. "Do you or do you not realize Harve and I are breaking up forever? *Infinitesimally!* All on account of my horrible family!"

Ma squinted at her painting. "The stork should have carried you to Buckingham palace, not to peasants like us. The tags must have got mixed!"

"Oh, *be* funny!" Francie rolled over some way and tumbled on the floor, ka-*bump!*

"Wha—WHOOP!" I laughed. I couldn't help it. Jill popped her hand over her mouth, but some snicks escaped.

Frances scrambled around, looking for her shoes. "All I want is for my family to be dignified!" she wailed. "Harve comes from a dignified family! And he's the most important athlete in school!"

"Then why doesn't he play better?" I said.

"Because of our fight!" She sat down and jammed her shoes on. "And he can't come over to make up because I've got the horriblest family and the horriblest father in town!"

Dad walked in, in time to hear that one. He had on a grim little smile. "Let's let other people say that," he said. "That hero of yours tripped over his own big feet today. He's got three of them, you know. If he does that Saturday, we'll lose. And the town will tell you what kind of father you've got. You won't have to tell the town!"

"How can Harve play when you keep telling him you'll fire him?" Francie howled.

"I won't fire him," Dad said, in a strangled voice. "Awkward or no, he made four TD's in scrimmage.

So if we lose tomorrow, I'll just be pleased to very happily resign!"

Kristan stood there, gasping. "Frances, *please* look up 'infinitesimally'! And your grammar—"

"I use excellent grammar, in my mind," Francie said, with her chin up and her eyes half closed.

Kris turned to Dad. "And, Daddy—"

"Dinner's about ready!" Mom said quickly. "Ten minutes!"

Dad went and kissed Mom and ran upstairs.

"Set the table, Jill, dear," Mom said. "And it won't be easy. Frances, time *is!*"

Frances has just one job at our house—dishes. Ma says we really shouldn't ask a princess to do more, and anyway it's the only job she ever seems to get done. So Ma is firm. Nobody helps. If Francie lets the dishes go until there are no clean ones, we simply eat on second-hand ones. She had let them go.

"I'll manage," Jill said. She grabbed me and whispered, "Mom made apple pie! The minute Daddy tastes it I'll ask for the ten dollars!"

Dinner the night before the game is always rough. We try to discuss something else.

Kristan sighed. "Did you hear Webber playing Brahms? Mr. Spencer told Mrs. Burnside that Webber's vibrato is astonishing. Webber will one day be the finest violinist in West Comet, and concertmaster in Symphonette, and—"

"Is John Spencer going to move over?" Mom asked.

"Well, when he becomes senile, of course!" Kris said. "I mean, he has been a great credit to West Comet—

28

a man who has been a concert violinist and will deign to settle in a small town, teach talented young musicians, and—well, accept civic responsibilities. But one has one's day, doesn't one? And don't you suppose that, besides being quite lame, he's almost forty? I'm sure he wouldn't keep a young musician down. I'm sure he'll *know* when he's senile! And when Webber is ready!"

Mostly, Kris has good sense. But she had such an awful case on that fat creep, Webber Burnside, that it was actually disgusting, and when she talked about him she looked almost beautiful.

Dad was gazing at her, kind of fascinated. He can't stand Webber's practicing when he is charting plays.

Jill pulled at his sleeve. "Daddy?"

"Yup?" He grinned. The apple pie was very good. "That's me!"

"Daddy, Eric needs ten dollars, to be a ham radio operator."

Dad looked surprised. "That's great, Skipper! Takes brains!"

I talked fast. "Dad, I need a code practice set. I mean, I'll make it. And I need an old radio with a shortwave band."

"You see, Daddy," Jill said, "there's nothing—absolutely nothing like having a ham in the family!"

Mom nodded. "That's what the hams' mothers keep telling me. I'd hate to miss it!"

Dad was reaching to his money pocket, when Kris had to speak up again. "Daddy, my conscience forces me to bring up something that was interrupted. The

29

older one grows, the more careful one should learn to be. Especially when one wishes to keep one's position of authority."

Up came the hand. It hadn't been inside the money pocket. "Go on!"

"Well, you said, 'That's me,' just now. And a while ago you split your infinitive."

"No!" Dad exclaimed. "I'm *sorry!* In my mind, I use excellent grammar!" He winked at Ma and she almost burst with a held-back laugh, and Dad began to reach for the money again.

But Kristan had to go on. "It was when you said, 'I'll be pleased to very happily resign.'"

My hope died a revolting death. Up came Dad's hand. Fist, rather. "Kris." He half whispered. He rapped the fist on the table without a sound. "All of you! Kindly forget what I say in this house and don't quote me outside it! If we lose tomorrow's game, can't you see it in the *Clarion?* 'Coach Andy ready to throw in the sponge! The head of West Comet High's athletic department spoke openly of resigning Saturday. . . .'"

"I'm sorry!" Kris was blushing.

The doorbell rang. Dad sprang up and started toward the door. He looked back. "Frances, I've got my boosting foot ready! If you've told Bonner he can come here tonight—*I* told him to be beddy-bye at nine—Oh, hello, Mattie!"

"Good evening, Andy!" Mrs. Burnside bustled in. She is a quite big lady with lots of brown hair piled up on top of her head. She has kind of big eyes and eyebrows and a kind of big voice. Sometimes she comes to reform

31

me, sometimes to brag about Webber, sometimes to make Betsy come home, or other things. This time it was to check on Ma's art.

She looked at the painting on the easel. "Oh, *Hilda!*" She shook her head. "You're getting nowhere! If you'd only decide what it is you're painting! I just know the Ingeborg Bloomer Colony won't have a decent showing at the exhibit! The city women will think—"

I escaped to the kitchen. Jill came along. "Eric," she whispered, "you've got six dollars. I've got three. And I'll get something out of Kris for spoiling things."

I don't know what I'd do without Jill! "I'll pay it back when the snow comes," I said. "I want to cinch that radio before that fellow sells it to someone else. Thanks—Butch!"

She beamed. I call her Butch sometimes, and nothing makes her happier.

Bill Adkins brought the radio to Charlie's, Saturday morning. Mike Miller and Don Bishop were along. "You're getting a good buy," they assured me. "Most guys start with one of these."

"Eric's getting parts for a code practice set," Charlie told them. "I'm going down to Mean John's with him this morning."

Bill grinned. "Watch your shirt at Mean John's," he said.

Charlie and I had some cookies and hurried down to Front Street, to Mr. Spencer's Electrical and Metal Supply Store. "I don't get this 'Mean John' bit," I said. "Mr. Spencer's always keen when Pa buys stuff from him."

"Ya," Charlie said. "Boy, you've got it all to learn!"

A bell on the door jingled as we went inside.

Mr. Spencer is a thin man, quite lame. He has thick, black hair and very dark, keen eyes. He was sitting back of a counter, copying a music score and humming, just as he was the last time Dad and I went in.

I said just what Dad said. "Good morning! Getting ready for the next concert?"

He looked up and his face seemed to freeze. He looked as if he had never seen a more unwelcome sight in his whole life.

He got up slowly. "Well? Let's get it over with."

I shook, but Charlie said, "Mr. Spencer, Eric wants to be a ham."

"All right! Get on with it!"

My face was hot. I almost melted into my shoes. Here was one more person who hated me.

He turned his back and began digging in some drawers under his shelves. He had on a light blue shirt and black pants, and he always wears a tie. And although he lived alone in the rooms back of the store, he always looked as if somebody just pressed his pants and he hadn't sat down in them yet. There was never a wrinkle on him anywhere.

He was jawing. "OK. You want to shake me down for some old wire for an antenna."

I poked Charlie. "Let's go!"

"Shut up!" Charlie hissed. "It kills him if you go."

"Well, hurry up!" Mean John yelled. "What else?"

"Sir—" Charlie hitched up his pants and swung on one foot.

Mean John growled, "If you want something, order it. If you're going to dance, hire a stage!"

Charlie went right on. "Eric has to make his own code practice set."

"Why?" Mean John yelled. "Just why does Coach Andy Crane's only son have to make his own code practice set? I'll answer that! So he can torture the *soul* out of me!"

"No, sir," I stammered. "I c-can't ask Dad when—"

Charlie poked me and said, "We need a high frequency buzzer. I guess we've got batteries."

"Sure. You'll rob a flashlight or two!"

"We need some screws," Charlie said. "And a telegraph key and connectors."

"I *know* what you need!" Mean John yelled.

He did, too. Scared as I was, I noticed he put things down on the counter before Charlie told him.

"That'll be three-forty!" He folded his arms and glared at me.

I counted the money. "One, two, two-fifty, three, three-thirty, thirty-three—" I almost died. "That's all I brought!"

"Some mathematician! Some grades you must get!" Mean John said. "Here! You gave me thirty-three cents too much."

"Sir, you s-said three-forty—"

"Three dollars! Now take that junk and get out of here!"

"Yes, sir," I said. "Th-thanks."

"Why?" he yelled. "You *paid* me, didn't you?"

I shook. But Charlie didn't seem bothered. He poked

down the length of the store, looking at hardware and electrical things.

Near the door there was a grandfather clock and also a cabinet with a glass door. The door was padlocked.

Charlie pointed. "Ha! There's where Bill Adkins' camera went! I *thought* so!"

"His camera?" It was Bill's camera, all right. I gawked. I saw a fishing reel that I recognized, and Mike Miller's knife. There was a watch with the band almost worn off, and a pen and a catcher's mitt and other things.

The clock began to chime, and right then Mean John got us by the necks. "I said, get *out* of here!"

We got.

When I could talk, I did. "Charlie, what did I *do?*"

"Not a thing," Charlie grinned. "Mean John's always like that to the fellows. But—he is a very good guy."

"Good guy? What about Bill's camera, and that other stuff?"

"Oh, that's one of Mean John's great kindnesses," Charlie said. "If a ham can't pay for something he needs, he can leave some piece of property there with Mean John and redeem it when he's able."

"That mitt was Don Bishop's," I said. "I could see his initials."

Charlie laughed. "Oh, Don owes his soul to Mean John," he said. "Just like that song. So do most of the guys."

"Well, *I* won't!"

"Hah!" Charlie laughed. "Just give yourself time!"

36

A Balcony Is Wasted on a Boy

At my house, Ma was cleaning the back hall. Mrs. Burnside was there, advising her. "Hilda, this is nonsense! You missed a streak, there. No, dear, that blue square. The back hall isn't important, when your painting isn't done."

"You know I can't paint when Andy has a game," Ma said.

"Excuse me,"I said.

"Excuse me," said Charlie.

Mrs. Burnside moved just a little. She said, "Webber has been practicing since eight o'clock."

"That's sure nice, Mrs. Burnside," I said. "Webber was playing that soonata with hardly any squeaks this morning. Excuse me!"

We pushed past without bumping her.

"It's sonata," she said. Well, my piano teacher has told me that.

Kris was running the sweeper in the dining room. Francie was on the window seat in her rollers and her blue shirttail. Dad named it a shirttail. It's a long wrapper of some kind, and we see a lot of it. Francie wears some blue feather floppy slippers with it, when she can find them.

She had greasy goo all over her face, and she was polishing her nails. A magazine was propped up in front of her, and she was trying to turn the pages without smudging her nail polish.

"Hey, Kris!" I yelled. "Where's Jill?"

Kris turned off the sweeper and Francie howled. "See what you did to my nails!"

"We didn't touch your nails!" I said.

"You yelled. You know I'm jumpy when Harve and Daddy have a game!"

"If Dad lets Harve play," I said. "Where's Jill?"

The polish smelled. Francie's goo smelled. Something that was cooking smelled. But Kristan sniffed at us. "What's in those hardware bags that smells questionable?"

"Just—something questionable," I said. "If Jill comes, tell her we took my up to my shack."

"You took your—what?" Kris shouted. "Where?"

But we were halfway upstairs, snickering. Around the corner in the upstairs hall, I stopped to pick up some of Francie's underwear and toss it down the chute. She's always dropping something like that, and she never goes back to pick it up.

We went to my room and Charlie said, "You've got a little problem here."

"I know. There's not much room."

Charlie opened my closet door. "Know what? You could hang your good pants and jacket and things on the head of your bed and put your good shoes and tennies under it, and move your desk into the closet."

"There wouldn't be room for any other ham," I said.

"That's so." He went to the other door. "The shake porch," he said.

"Yes. I wish it wasn't in my room. Kristan's on it half the time, shaking mops and dust rags."

"Hasn't anybody got a big closet?" Charlie asked.

"Mom and Dad, downstairs. And Francie, up here. I'll show you."

In Francie's room we had to go stepping over things and getting caught in things. I said, "A princess always has a lady to make her bed and pick up her underwear and vac up the powder and hair rinse envelopes and feathers and toenails from her floor. Francie has a lady, but she is scrubbing the back hall right now. Although Kris sneaks in with the sweeper." I opened the closet door. "Here!"

"Oh, boy! Oh, man!" Charlie almost drooled. "A great big walk-in closet, with two windows and room for a big operating desk and three or four chairs! Eric— would Francie trade?"

"Not a chance—unless Jill could con her into it."

Suddenly Charlie clapped his hands over his ears. "Eee-ow! I don't know! You'd have to put up with *that!*"

"Right!" I said. "Webber's room is just across the driveway, and he practices two hours every day."

"With the window open?"

"In summer he practices on that porch. Jeeps, Charlie, don't stand in the window with your hands on your ears and that look of terrible pain on your face!"

"It's an honest look," Charlie said.

"Sure. But Mrs. Burnside is very touchy when people are honest about Webber's music. Watch him now! He's finishing that soonata!"

Webber drew a long, long bow, with his eyes closed, looking real holy. Then he made a deep bow to his audience, which was a lamp with the shade on crooked.

"Snick!" said Charlie. He clapped.

Maybe Webber heard him. He put down his violin and closed his window and left his room.

"Suppose he'll come over to complain?" Charlie wondered.

"If he comes over to cut our heads off, Kris will be happy," I grinned. "Just so he comes! But he won't!"

We went back to my room. Charlie said, "Let's move your desk over beside the window. That's where your antenna will come in."

We moved the desk. It was pretty close to my bed. "That's OK," I said. "I can sit right on the side of the bed to work."

"A lot can be done with a bed," Charlie said. "You can use it for a work table. And a healthy guy can always sleep on the floor." He patted my patchwork quilt. "This won't show dirt and stuff. My ma got me that yellow bedspread and told me to keep it clean." He moaned.

"I'm between bedspreads, since my chemistry accident," I said.

Charlie looked in my desk. "When the drawers get full of ham stuff, the books and dictionary can go under your bed. And you can make a box cupboard. Mean John gets hold of keen wooden boxes. What you do is, you stand outside—well, I'll go with you when the time comes. Right now, let's put your code practice set together. You got a manual?"

"Not yet." I needed everything.

"Mr. Kirby will loan you a manual," Charlie said. "Oh, you'll get along, Eric. Mike Miller started out in his garage, until he froze his toe."

"I remember," I said. "He's got the attic now. All fixed with plasterboard. It's real keen."

"You'll get something, too," Charlie said. "Because all parents know that there's absolutely nothing like having a ham in the house."

"Ma knows it," I said. "But very few guys have athletic coach dads who they've flunked out on."

"Eric Crane!" We jumped. Kris was behind us, looking shocked. "What have you done to your room, and how can we get at it to clean it? I can't even see the floor between your bed and desk!"

"What you can't see won't hurt you," I said.

She didn't hear me. "And *'who he's flunked out on'!* Eric Crane, if you flunk English—"

I'll be honest. Kristan cares. In a way, Kris runs our place. Mom has her hands full, trying to keep the coach bucked up and the market under control and Mrs. Burnside off her neck. Kris seems to think Francie is retarded. She picks up after her and waits on her. You'd swear she was older than the Princess, instead of a year younger. Jill looks out for herself and me, but Kris is a real big sister to her, too.

Now she sighed. "Well—lunch is almost ready."

Dad doesn't eat at home on game days, even when the game's in town. This one wasn't, but even so, game-day meals are terrible, especially if Dad won't let the girls go to the game.

41

The radio blared. "The West Comet Comets are on the field. There's Bill Glenn, George Adamski, Marv Vincent, the fullback. There's Pete Manders, the Whitney twins, Bob and Rick—identical, that is . . ."

"I don't care whether he plays or not!" Francie said, meaning Harve.

"Frances—that *shrimp!*" Kris said. Francie passed her the butter.

"Freddie Shinners gets a hand . . ."

"Who *cares?*" Jill whispered. Her shoulders were hunched up and her eyes were squeezed tight. We were all hoping—except Francie, of course, that Dad would let old Harve play.

The announcer went on. "Carl Sheldon, Russ Williamson, Johnny Whipp . . ." A pause, the longest in history. He had named ten men.

"Ugh!" Kristan shuddered. *"Frances!"*

"I just hope Daddy doesn't relent," Francie said. She took a gulp of cocoa. Mom reached over and very gently took her cup.

"Here's the quarterback in this day's game," the announcer said. "He gets a hand—this big, red-haired junior! Number seventeen—Harve Bonner!"

Jill and I whooped.

"Oh!" Kristan sighed. "Oh! *Oh!* Thank heaven!"

"I knew Daddy would let him play," Francie said. "I was perfectly cool and collected." She reached. "What—where's my cocoa?"

"Honey," Mom said, "you'll have to start over. You were so cool and collected that you dropped three shrimps in the first cup!"

Listening to Dad's games, I always get a dry mouth. I just plain forget to shut it. The score at the half was West Comet 10, Almeda 7.

"Coach Andy will be giving his boys a talk, you can bet!" the announcer said. "Andy has his eye on the championship this year!"

The final score was West Comet 35, Almeda 15.

Jill moaned. "Daddy won't call that good enough!"

The *Clarion* was out before Dad got home. "Look at this vulgar sports page!" Kristan scolded.

Although he will not come home exactly upon his shield, Coach Andy Crane had little that was good to say for his Comets after today's game. "A few touchdowns and conversions, and Almeda would have licked us!" he moaned, dabbing his eyes. "It wasn't championship playing. And yet—" The saddest coach managed a weak smile. "Don't say I'm a defeatist. . . ."

The telephone rang. Jill got it. "For you, Francie."

"It's that drip, Sidney Temple!" Jill hissed. "Tell him to get lost!"

Francie drifted to the phone. "Tonight?" she said. "No . . . No, I'm not busy . . . Well, I guess . . . For a while . . . OK."

She hung up and looked at us. "Sid's coming over and bringing his guitar."

"That's treason!" I gasped.

"Yes, it is!" Kris said. "Frances, what would you do if you were engaged to a boy who had to go to war? Mother, isn't this treason?"

Ma considered. "Keep Sid out of Dad's hair, Francie."

Dad can't stand Sid Temple, and there is a very good reason besides his looks, which are quite sissy. Whenever Harve and Francie fight, Sid seems to be poking his pointed nose around a corner somewhere, so that he knows it and calls Frances up. Then he comes over and plays that guitar and howls. Dad can't understand one word he sings. And the way Sid grins when he's singing makes Dad sick. Also, Harve gets temperamental when this happens, and scrimmage goes badly.

"All right!" Francie said. "Do you dream I would have chosen this? Nay, never! But Harve's in football, he'll be in basketball, he'll be in track! And with Daddy's curfews, I'll *never* see him! So—can I just sit home and let Harve think he is the only man who admires me? Can I? Do you know I haven't heard one word from him since Thursday? *One word?*"

"Since you hung up on him!" I said.

"That's Daddy's fault!" Francie wailed.

Right then Dad got home. He strode in with a funny little grin on his face. "I'm home," he said. "Bearing my shield!" He kissed Ma, and turned to Francie. "Well, honey, what did you think of Harve?"

"I was very happy for him, that you let him play," Francie said.

"Let him play!" Dad laughed. "I told him to get in there and produce, or I'd boost him into the middle of next week!"

Francie screamed. "Daddy! What will Harve's mother think?"

Francie says Harve's mother is particular, even

though Kris has seen her buy a utility grade beef roast. Harve's name is not Harvey. It is Harvard, because his mother knew when he was born that he is going to go to Harvard, although his dad thinks not.

"She ought to feel OK tonight," Dad said. He hugged Kris and Jill and felt my shoulder for a muscle. "You're looking meatier, Skipper." He meant meatier than when he first began to get worked up over the Almeda game. He winked. "We'll surprise Durbin next fall. A guy with a chance at Mother's cooking can't lose! You get that code practice set?"

"Sure, Pa!"

"You might show a fellow."

We sprinted upstairs. "This is it, Dad! Look! I'm starting code." I tapped. "Here's A!" I pounded out E and I and S and H and 5. "I'm slow," I said.

"You'll master it. Say, you made a good set!"

"Thanks, Dad!"

But I knew what he wished, and I wished with all my heart I had made the team. So I let him go without telling him I was up for a loan.

When Sid arrived I phoned Charlie. "Could we go to Mr. Kirby's tonight, and ask him if he'll help me?"

"You bet! Got your bike?"

"You know my bike's O.O.O. We can walk."

"A mile?" Charlie said. "Oh, no! You trot too fast. I'll take you on my handlebars."

So that was how I first went to Mr. Kirby's.

He was in his living room, watching TV with Mrs. Kirby. He's a real keen man, quite tall, with a mustache. He is West Comet's postmaster.

"So you want to be a ham, Eric!" he said. "Great!"

I took a deep breath. There wasn't a word about how he'd supposed Andy's son would be busy with football.

"Have you a code practice outfit?"

"Yes, sir. Charlie and I made it."

He looked at me sharply then. "Your dad doesn't— object?"

"Oh, no, sir. He doesn't care."

Mr. Kirby's shack used to be a den. It had a fireplace and a rug. His rig was on a table built against the wall. The walls were paneled with wood, and one end was covered with QSL cards.

Charlie pointed to some letters on a card. "See this W.A.S., Eric? That means this ham has worked all states. So has Mr. Kirby."

Mr. Kirby nodded. "That's right. It means a ham has talked with a ham in every state in the Union. Arizona was the tough one for me. I began to think there was no ham in Arizona, or even that there was no Arizona! You have a license manual, Eric?"

"No, sir."

"Here." He took one from a drawer. "You borrow this. Done any practicing?"

"A little, with Charlie, sir."

"Let's hear a few letters. Use this key."

I pounded off E, I, S, H and 5. He nodded. "Very good. You'll have a good fist. For now, you work on that same group. Get away from the chart. Learn your code by sound. Do lots of listening. And come up with Charlie Tuesday night." He smiled. "Your dad happy about the game?"

"Well, you saw what the paper said. But I think he's happy."

As Charlie wheeled me homeward I remembered something in Mr. Kirby's shack that had puzzled me. "It looked like another set, but smaller."

"Oh, that's his battery-powered transceiver," Charlie said. "For emergencies. Electricity could fail, you know."

I nodded. "Just about anything can fail," I said.

By Monday the market was low. The Morton game was coming up and Harve was grounded and Sid Temple phoned Francie again.

We got to talking about it in Fords' on Wednesday. We were getting a soda—Charlie and Jill and Betsy and I. Harve was down at the fountain all alone.

"I would *die* if we got Sid Temple in the family," Jill said.

"Me, too," I agreed.

"Then we've got to encourage Harve some way. He thinks Francie's through! And after the way Daddy treats him—well, come *on*, before he leaves!"

So we walked over and Charlie started to encourage Harve. "Hi, Harve! Did you know Francie's going to Sid Temple's hootenanny?"

Betsy stood on Charlie's foot.

Harve's face got red as his hair. "I heard about it."

"Of course, Harve," Jill said, "you can really play the guitar better than Sid and sing better, too."

Harve agreed. "Sid sings through his nose."

Betsy sighed. "Francie is such a—a princess, Harve."

"Um-huh," Harve said. "That's right."

"She's like a princess in an—an enchanted tower," Jill said. "The kind that would love a troubador, singing beneath her balcony—"

"In the pale, sweet moonlight," Betsy sighed. "Play on the strings of my heart!" She looked at me. Betsy gives me some looks sometimes that worry me. Of course, she *is* the best Burnside.

"Moonlight," Harve said. "Well, when a guy has to get all his night life in before moonrise—" Suddenly he grinned and winked. He took a last drag on the milk shake. "See you!" he said, and hurried out.

At seven o'clock I was coming home from Charlie's, wishing I had a shack of my own, when I heard this plink-plink! There was Harve, all dressed up, standing under my shake porch singing his heart out.

"I'll always be around, if you nee-eed me . . ."

Mrs. Burnside poked her head out her front door. "Eric!" she called softly. "For heaven's sake, what ails Harvard?"

Then it happened. The shake porch door opened. Someone flew out. A mop banged over the railing and a shower of *everything* began to fall all over Harve. Man, was he astonished! And was I!

It was a cloud of dust in big, fluffy rolls, and there was string in it, and hair and paper and feathers and everything. Poor old Harve looked up and got it in his eyes and mouth. He began to bat at this stuff the way you would bat at bees.

"Hey!" he yelled. "What's the idea?"

I ran inside. "Ma!" I called. "Who's shaking the dust mop?"

49

Everyone was yelling. Francie was screaming across the room in her shirttail. "Oh, I've got the terriblest family! What will Harve's mother think, now?"

Dad had been in the den charting plays. He was standing in the den door yelling. "What brought that big lummox here?"

Mom was calling up the stairs. "Jill! Jill! Call Kristan!"

Francie wailed, "I'll never speak to Kristan Crane again as long as I live!"

"Look!" I said. "It's all my fault!"

"Yours!" Francie shrieked. "I should have known!" She flopped to the window. "Oh, there he goes! I'll never see him again!" She collapsed on the sofa and tried to die.

"Why is it your fault, Eric?" Mom said.

"Well, my room. Quite a few things got collected under my bed, and I suppose Kris saw her chance. Look. She didn't know Harve was there!"

Francie sat up and wept. "Harve thought the shake porch was my balcony! He thought that was my room! So he—he did something sweet! And see what he got! Oh—whoo-whoo-whoo—BAW!"

"Harve's head's on crooked," Dad said.

Kristan was coming down the stairs looking dazed. She still had the mop in her hands and I don't think she knew it. She kind of pointed it at us. "I—I'm sorry!" she said. "My intentions were unimpeachable! Irreproachable! Jill said Frances was phoning Dot Speaker, so it would be a good time to clean her room—"

"Francie's room!" Dad said.

51

And Mom began to laugh. "Forgive me, Francie! I—
I can't help it! I—I'll help you. But, *oh!*" She put her
head against Dad's sleeve and laughed and cried until
she was weak. Dad looked at her with that funny,
puzzled, fascinated look.

Kris stood on the stairs like a statue, gaping at him.
Suddenly Francie rushed up past her and disappeared.

Ma wiped her eyes and went to the phone and dialed.
We heard her say, "You come over, Harve, when you
get brushed off. . . . I know, but I said you may come.
. . . Yes, curfew is lifted, tonight. . . . I know, but *I* say
it's all right." She hung up and smiled at Dad.

All he said was, "What's the commotion upstairs?"

Francie stood at the top of the stairs with her arms
full of clothes. "I'm moving out!" she shrieked. "That
—*did* it!"

She disappeared. We were speechless. I couldn't
breathe.

In a minute she was back at the top of the stairs
with her arms full of different clothes. Very different!
They were mine! And Jill was beside her, with an arm-
load of my things.

Francie looked down at us and yelled, "I've always
wanted a balcony! A balcony is wasted on a boy! He
doesn't even know what it's for! So Mister Eric Crane
is trading rooms with me—as of tonight—whether he
likes it or not!"

Everybody drew a deep breath. Mine was deepest.
I had my shack!

I glanced carefully at Jill. She grinned—the happiest grin in the world—and winked at me.

Walk Right Into My Shack

Well, I had a shack. I put my receiver on a black table that I hauled up from the basement. This left room for four red plastic chairs from an old set of Ma's. Charlie Korth helped me string my wire out in the hickory tree. I put a KEEP OUT sign on the door, for drips.

All the guys came over to see. Hank Thomas patted my receiver. "Mark Bickford had this once. He got it from Mr. Peterman. It's a very good starting set. And you've got a keen shack, Eric."

Everyone agreed.

We all went over to Mr. Kirby's. He was very delighted to hear about my shack, and as long as we were there he drilled us on code. He pounded out words and sentences and we copied.

"Wait!" I gasped, once. "Back there I missed—"

"Never mind what you miss. Just get what you can." We knew he was trying not to make it too hard. No hour ever went faster.

At home I went right to my shack and tuned around until I found some code I could copy. Again, time went fast. At ten o'clock I looked up and it was half past eleven, and Kristan was at my door.

"Eric, that racket! It was very distracting while I was writing my theme!" That's one thing against my shack. It's next door to her room. No privacy for me.

"OK," I said, "can't you read signs?"

"Signs?"

"Namely, the one on that door. K-E-E-P O-U-T!"

Kris actually looked embarrassed. "You m-might put *please* on it!"

"Aw, it's for drips and creeps, not for you," I said. "I don't say please to drips and creeps."

She thought that over.

"Don't look now, Kris," I said, "but Webber can see you."

"Webber!" She stepped back into my bedroom. She had on a white sweater and black slacks, but she had rollers on her hair. I smelled shampoo.

"Who else?" I said. "He's been peeking in here all evening."

"Because your noise disturbed his studying!"

"With my windows shut? Oh, no! But curiosity killed a cat, and old Webber must be part Angora. I'd better quit, before we see a fat boy's name in the obit column."

"Webber is not fat!"

"And he can't hear my clicking!"

"I can hear that radio!"

"That will stop when I get earphones," I said. "Signing off! Which means this conversation is ended and I expect no response."

I got one though. As Kris strode back through my room I heard it. "That *horrible* patchwork quilt!"

Dad was getting geared for a tough Crandon game, so Kris didn't start anything at breakfast. "But she

won't forget," I told Charlie, when we went to school. "And she's definitely off my list of people who like me!"

"A ham *has* to listen in the night," Charlie said. "You need earphones. Tell your dad—"

"Not before Crandon!" I said. "Not on report card day!"

I got home just as Ma signed Kristan's card. "This calls for a little extra bonus, dear!" Mom kissed her.

"Kris make the honor roll?" I said. "Hey! Keen! Congratulations!"

"And when have I failed to make the *high* honor roll?" Kris asked me very coldly. "I have that dread experience to look forward to—next time!"

"Now, what brings this on?" Ma said.

"The racket from Eric's radio! It even kept Webber awake last night! He was half asleep in geometry today!"

Jill spoke up. "Only half? Big day! Kris, Webber couldn't possibly hear Eric's radio!"

"TNX, Jill," I grinned.

Kristan gasped. " 'TNX'? What does that mean?"

"That's a ham's thanks." Jill blushed because she was so proud that she knew. "Don't be so ignorant!" she told Kris. "When you live in the same house with a ham, there's no excuse for being so ignorant!"

I don't know what I'd do without Jill!

"Here's my card, Mom," I said. "Sign here. Right here."

"I'll examine it first, please," Ma said. "Stop pulling on it. What's this?"

"Where?" I said. "Just a speck of—"

"Right here, Mister!" Ma said. "In the math square."

"Oh, that!" I said. "That looks like B-Minus, Ma. Good old B-Minus. Next best to a B, if you've been very busy."

"Any movement on that one had better be upward," Mom said. She signed the card and I got away.

I could hear Kris. "Mother! Aren't you going to limit his time at that radio? Would Mrs. Burnside just sign that inferior card and—"

"As you know," Ma said, "I didn't finish my painting for the exhibition. I let the Ingeborgs down. In Mrs. Burnside's book I'm an unfit mother and in the dog-house!"

Kristan wailed. "Mother! What an obscene expression!"

I got my allowance Friday. "You getting earphones?" Charlie asked.

"Nope! I'm getting a bicycle tire. Jill is contributing, and I'll pay her back when the snow comes."

"But—you *need* earphones!"

"I can see another way to get them," I said. "It may take a while."

I was pretty busy. I had to raise the math grade. The trouble was, I studied in my shack after school and the receiver and the code practice set were right there. Also, some evenings I went to Charlie's or some other ham's house. Or Charlie and the guys came over, and we practiced sending and copying code. It was great fun.

"Mr. Kirby's going to think we're getting good," Charlie said on Tuesday, when he stopped for me.

"I wish all our teachers were just like him," I said. "I wish Mr. Painter was like him, in math!"

"Hams are different," Charlie said.

I rode my bike over to Mr. Kirby's, but I knew the other tire was going.

"When your dad won the last game you should have asked for another tire," Charlie said.

I moaned. "The market's down now. Pa says Anston will beat him."

"He always says that."

Well, Dad never brags. A coach is always quoted, especially if he brags. And a very bad headline is COACH SOMEBODY EATS CROW!

"Personally," my dad always says, "nobody has learned to cook crow any way that suits me."

"Dad's installing the door for me tomorrow," Charlie told me. "I forgot and slammed the doors last night, trotting back and forth from my bedroom to my shack. I woke Dad up." He squinted at me. "You're lucky your dad sleeps downstairs."

I had thought of that. A coach gets very little sleep, and what he gets cannot be disturbed. "If Dad slept upstairs I couldn't be a ham," I said. "It's bad enough, being next door to Kris."

"And across the drive from Webber Burnside!"

I grinned. "That could pay off!"

Mr. Kirby drilled six of us on our code that night. "Listen and copy a lot," he said. "And practice sending. You only have to send and copy five words a minute for your first exam. Which reminds me. Better start thinking about those transmitters!"

I was in my shack at ten o'clock when Jill tiptoed in. "Aren't you listening, Eric?"

"I'm just sitting here, worrying about my transmitter," I said. "Charlie thinks I'll need around thirty dollars for parts I can't scrounge. Has anyone asked you what I want for Christmas?"

"Not yet." Jill shook her head. Her hair swung. "Wait! Betsy did!"

"I meant the family," I said. Betsy gave me a key chain last year, so Ma made me give her a record. I said, "Tell the family that I want money for my big gift."

At our house everybody gets one big present from the family, something he chooses and wants. Also, everybody gets some little surprise gifts that aren't supposed to cost much.

"What about your little gifts?" Jill asked.

"Money," I said. "And for my birthday—money!"

I don't get much for my birthday, anyway, as it's too soon after Christmas. Jill does better. Hers is before Christmas.

"I'll tell everyone," she said. "Oh! And about my birthday, Eric—"

"Yes?" I *had* to give Jill a birthday present!

"I got myself two records from you," she said. "You can pay me when the snow comes."

"Thanks!" I said. "TNX, YL!"

She giggled. "Signing off!" She closed the door.

God sure knew what he was doing when he sent Jill!

The next morning she earned seventy-five cents for

my fund. It was this way. Francie drifted downstairs in her blue shirttail and flopped into a chair. Kris brought her an egg and Jill put in some toast for her. I said. "How's Harve? Was he under your balcony last night?"

She looked at me with one eye. "No! He was under Daddy's *thumb!*" She poured some coffee and stared at it. "Mother, this is my cup from last night! Because I was wearing Frosted Rose lipstick—"

"Isn't it nice that you got the same cup, dear?" Mom smiled. "The girl who washes dishes here didn't report for work yesterday, and we've run out." Mom stopped smiling. "Time *was!*"

Francie looked extremely surprised and hurt. "You *know* I'm upset about Harve, and the games! Did you see the paper?"

Everyone had seen the sports page. The headline was:

CRY, THE BELOVED COACH!

The story began: *With the Sampson game looming and Harve Bonner possibly out with a sprained tendon, the inconsolable Andy Crane stood at his wailing wall today, loudly predicting that this is the time he'll come home upon his shield. . . .*

"I'm extremely upset," Francie repeated. "I'll wash dishes. But just when, I can't say. Nay, I cannot say!"

"I'll wash 'em, Francie!" Jill said. "For fifty cents!"

"Nay!" Ma said. "Seventy-five! In advance!"

Francie moaned. "Get my red purse!" It had been lost three days.

Jill went upstairs on the dead run and came down faster, with the purse. Francie fiddled and fumbled and sorted and sighed and picked coins. "Here's sixty-five," she said hopefully.

"*Seventy*-five," Ma said, "or no deal!"

"Well, *Mo*-ther!" Francie made her eyes look real big. "Honestly, if Harve's mother knew the Crane family quibbles over a dime—"

"Seventy-five, or you'll star in a story called 'The Princess and the Sink,'" Ma said.

Francie came up with a little coin purse that had a powder puff and two dimes in it. "Here!" she said. "Seventy-five, *if* we must be such peasants!"

"Yippee!" Jill grinned at me and shook her hands up over her head, and the doorbell rang.

"Mrs. Burnside," Ma sighed. "To tell me what the artists said about my painting, which defaulted."

Kris opened the door and gasped. "Good—good evening, Webber!"

"*Evening!*" I said. "Gosh, Kris, don't you know this is breakfast?"

Jill giggled. "Kris got confused because it's the supper dishes!"

"I was merely joking," Kris said, looking miserable.

Webber hadn't heard one word. He was standing there, squirming, in his maroon jacket and green pants, with his curly hair slicked down.

"I beg pardon?" he said.

Ma said, very gently, "Kristan said good morning. You remember Kristan, don't you, Webber? You used to play house with her."

61

Kris turned redder than Webber, and that was quite red. "Mother!" She tried to laugh. "You *know* we're in the same classes! Isn't it a lovely morning, Webber?"

He seemed to nod. "Mrs. Crane, I came—I mean, my mother came—I mean, my mother sent me to—" He looked at me. "Well, it's about some—a little—I mean, well, I'm supposed to practice for the Christmas recital and—well—" He made a very funny face. He opened his mouth and twisted it all around and closed it. He said, "You see, I practice in my room." He wiggled his fingers, as if he were fingering his violin. "And —well—my mother feels very concerned about distractions, so I—well—" He made that face again and looked up the stairs. "She said to tell you she's very concerned. About distractions."

Ma patted him. "Now, don't you worry! I'll tell your mother not to worry. Eric, why don't you show Webber your little room?"

"Sure!" I said, and Webber was upstairs before I was.

He hadn't been upstairs in our house for a couple years, since he got kind of grown up and quit knowing Kristan. But he sure knew I had a different room, and he pounced right through it to the door of my shack. There he stopped, staring at the sign.

"That's for creeps and jerks," I said. "And drips. Walk right into my shack, Webber."

"Shack?" he said.

"That's where a ham has his rig. His station. Have a chair!"

But Webber tiptoed over to my code practice set. "This is for code, isn't it?"

"Right! Mr. Spencer sold me the parts."

"He did?" Webber was pleased. "He's a very good guy."

Mean John.

"Oh, yes," I said. "A very good guy."

Webber smiled. He has some freckles, and for a minute he looked like a pretty good guy himself, and I noticed that he looks a little like Betsy.

Then he looked across at his window. "Well—Well—Mother said to get home and practice." He stopped at the door. "See you!"

"I *bet* you will!" I grinned. "See you!"

When I went downstairs, Ma was at the telephone. Kris was standing there, looking tragic, and Ma was saying, "That's right, Mattie. The poor boy came over to be sure his violin practice doesn't disturb Eric. Just tell him he doesn't disturb one bit! Tell him Eric is getting earphones, which shut out all other sounds. And if Webber's really worried, he can just close his window when he practices. Bye-bye, Mattie!"

Ma hung up and waved an envelope at me. It was marked: *Money for Earphones.*

"Thanks, Mom," I said. "I'll pay it back when the snow comes!"

"Mrs. Burnside will think we're stupid!" Kristan said. "Webber will never darken our door again!" Suddenly she choked and turned red. "That awful patchwork quilt! What did Webber say about that?"

"Nothing," I said. "My bed is kind of covered up with a few things. Webber never saw the quilt."

Kristan flew upstairs. We heard her scream.

"It's nothing alive, Ma," I said. "It's just wires and metal and some things I'm scrounging—I mean getting together. You can do a lot of things with a bed, Ma, and when I'm using mine for a worktable I just bunk on the floor."

"You—bunk on the floor?" Ma gasped.

"It's very soft, Ma. Don't worry. I'll get a box from Mean John—I mean Mr. Spencer—and make a cupboard."

Ma put her head down on her arms on the telephone desk and laughed. Anyway, I *think* she was laughing.

Something to Bawl About, Christmas

The earphones didn't end all my troubles! Mr. Painter muttered about my math grade.

"But," I told Charlie, "I've got so much on my mind, and on my bed. I haven't slept in it for three long nights."

"You need that box cupboard," Charlie said.

After school we went down to Mean John's. I was going in when Charlie stopped me. "Hold it! We go around to the back."

We went down the alley and found piles of cartons back of Mean John's door. "But these are cardboard!" I said.

"I know." Charlie smiled. "Start looking them over."

I had picked up just one when Mean John came to the back door. "What do you fellows want?" he yelled.

"Nothing," Charlie said.

"Well, you got it! Take it along!" The door slammed.

"Now," Charlie said, "start putting little cartons in one pile, big ones in another. Something like that."

We had made two piles when the door opened and Mean John yelled, "What in blazes do you fellows think you're doing?"

Charlie looked innocent. "Sorting discarded cartons, sir."

"I don't want them sorted!" Mean John yelled. "I

want them in an unsightly heap, just the way I threw them out!" The door banged.

"We'd better go, Charlie," I said.

"Oh, no! Now start tossing them back in one heap. Like this."

"You're getting them too close to the door," I said. "Mr. Spencer won't be able to open it."

"He's coming!" Charlie said. "Duck down behind the cartons!"

We ducked. The door opened. Out came a wooden box. Bam! "I warned you!" Mean John yelled. Out came three more. Bam! Bam! Bam! The door banged.

Charlie straightened up. He grinned. "They're dillies! Grab two and run, Eric. I'll use the others!"

"I feel like a thief," I said, as we ran. "Mr. Spencer didn't give us these boxes."

Charlie panted. "We can walk now."

We slowed down. "He gave us the boxes," Charlie said. "He wouldn't have sold them to us. Don Bishop tried to buy one once, and Mean John took the broom and put him out and threw the box after him. We always get them this way."

"Wouldn't it be more conventional if he gave them to us?"

"Then we'd thank him," Charlie said. "We'd be grateful. We'd act like we think he's not mean. That would kill him."

"But why?" I gasped.

Charlie said, "That's what nobody knows. Because he's Mean John, that's why. When the Ingeborg Bloomer Music and Art Colony ladies tell what a darling

John Spencer is, I turn sick. Because I know Mean John would be very ashamed. And he is a great guy."

When we lugged my boxes into our kitchen Ma was getting supper. She had on perfume and a yellow dress. My mother looks pretty in the kitchen.

Francie was trying to wash enough dishes for supper without getting her hands wet. Kris came, with one finger in her history book.

"Where did you get those things?" Kris demanded.

"From the alley," I said. "Back of Mean John's."

"The *alley!*" Francie gasped.

"Mean John!" Kris was horrified.

"You know Mr. John Spencer," I grinned. "Webber's violin teacher. He beaned us with them!"

Kris was gasping when we ran upstairs with the boxes. We snickered.

"You know," Charlie said, "your antenna isn't half long enough. You need fifty feet, at least."

"Mrs. Burnside would howl," I said.

"It's your hickory tree, isn't it?"

Well, I didn't have the wire.

But the next day after school Charlie said suddenly, "Jill's coming!"

Charlie has some funny sixth sense about Jill. He was right. She was right behind us with Betsy. They were excited. Betsy's cheeks were pink. In the sun her hair looked red-gold and shiny. I noticed she was getting taller, like Jill.

"Mr. Anderley's been remodeling," Jill said. "And it's junk night on Garfield Street, and—"

"Say no more!" Charlie said. "C'mon, Eric!"

We streaked back toward Garfield. I kept ahead of Charlie. Without bikes I can outrun any of the fellows.

"Mr. Anderley rewired!" Charlie told me, as he panted along. "I hope no other guys got there first!"

We planted our flag in Mr. Anderley's junk heap. "Boy!" Charlie said. "What a bonanza! We'll go through it, and leave what we reject in good order. Here's your antenna, Eric."

It was beautiful wire, at least seventy feet long. We coiled it and began sifting the other stuff.

We found switches and outlets and sockets and plugs and parts of light fixtures and a doorbell. "I wish we'd brought a basket," Charlie said. "Hey! There's your sister!"

I glanced around. "Hi, Francie!" I called. "Hi, Harve!"

Harve saluted. They were going home from school. Why they were on Garfield Street, don't ask me.

"Must be there's no scrimmage," I said. "Or Dad *did* can Harve!"

Charlie said, "Francie didn't see us."

"How could she help it?" I said. "She was afraid we'd ask them to help us carry this stuff home."

Just then Mr. Anderley came from his back-yard. "Find anything worth taking home?" he asked.

"Lots!" I said. "I have to make my transmitter."

"Reminds me," Mr. Anderley said. "When Eddie went back to college he left a transformer he wants to sell. He'll take three dollars."

"I'll buy it!" I said. "Mr. Anderley, I can leave you my wristwatch until I have the three dollars."

Mr. Anderley looked at me. He's a short man with quite a big stomach. He always smells like cigars. "I won't compete with Mean John," he said. "I think Eddie's still in hock to him. Tell you what! We'll just write an IOU on the wind, Eric."

"Just till the snow comes, Mr. Anderley," I said. "I'll do your walk until the transformer is paid for."

"It's a deal!" he said. "Say, I'll just back the car out. We'll load up your stuff in the trunk, and I'll drive you home."

Charlie helped string up the new antenna. Jill wanted to be the man in the tree, but I wouldn't allow that.

"Why not, Eric? I'm in slacks."

"Mrs. Burnside would come over to see if I was hanging you."

"She isn't watching!"

"Webber is," I said. "I'll go out in the hickory."

We got the antenna fixed and Charlie said, "Boy, that's going to help until you get your transmitter. You'll want a better one then."

We could smell supper. Jill poked me and pointed at Charlie.

"Can you stay?" I asked him.

"I've got to eat at home," he said. "Grandma's coming. But it's going to be late, so I'll stay up here and try out the new antenna."

Francie wasn't at the supper table. At dessert time I said, "Where's the Princess?"

"She has a headache," Kris told me.

Well, Francie has lots of headaches, and it looked as if there would be quite a few dishes to do.

I told the family about Mr. Anderley. "Boy, is he a wonderful guy! He's like Mr. Spencer. I mean, Mr. Spencer is a great guy, too, in a very mean way. They make a fellow think he wants to be like them!"

Pa was listening. Even with the market down and the Kimberly game looming, Pa was listening. I hoped he didn't get the wrong impression. If there's a man in the world I wish I could be like, it's my dad.

"I mean," I said, "I mean—Jeeps, Dad! I don't look much more like a football coach than I did in September!"

"I was going to work you out, Skipper," Dad said. "But I've been so blasted busy."

"Me, too," I said. "Fixing up the shack."

"Say!" Pa said suddenly. "Are you *ever* going to show me that shack?"

I whooped. "How about right now?"

"It's a deal!" Dad got up. "Excuse us, Mother?"

"And excuse me," Kristan said. "I'll fix a tray for Francie."

Dad stopped and stared around the table. He hadn't heard the conversation about Francie. He hadn't even missed her, because he was thinking about the game. "Where *is* Francie?" he said.

Ma sighed. "In her bower with a headache."

"She says she had a traumatic experience today," Kris explained.

"Traumatic!" Pa began to bark. "Has Francie been in an accident? Is she hurt? I know you keep things from me—"

"She is not hurt—visibly," Mom said.

72

Kris said, "She wouldn't talk. She probably scrapped with Harve."

"I let old Romeo off this afternoon with a sprained eyewinker," Dad said. "I suppose Francie had been shaking Sid Temple at him. The boy was so absent-minded we were better off without him."

"C'mon, Dad!" I said.

Ma was saying something. I half heard it, but it didn't register. I didn't think about it again until one o'clock in the morning, and then I almost died.

But right now I was just tickled because Pa wanted to see my shack.

Charlie was still at my receiver. Did he ever look surprised when my dad walked in! He was polite enough to stand up, but he gaped so that I could have bopped him.

"Dad came to have a look at the shack," I said.

"Mr. Crane, Eric will be needing his transmitter," Charlie said quickly. "He can scrounge all but about thirty—"

"That's fine!" Dad said. "Fine!" He looked at the box cupboard.

"I made that from boxes Mr. Spencer heaved at me," I said. I brushed some of Mr. Anderley's stuff off a chair. "Sit down, Pa."

Pa sat down and looked around. "I'd forgotten these walls are yellow."

"They'll be papered with QSL cards," Charlie said.

"QSL cards?"

I explained. "I have a long way to go before I'll be getting any."

73

"So this is the shack!" Dad nodded. "Skipper, it is great! Really great! You're doing all right! Have you got a shack, Charlie?"

"Yes, sir. I'd be happy to show you."

"When I get over there after the season, you remind me," Dad said. He looked at his watch and got up. His hand was warm on my shoulder, feeling for muscles. "I wish I could stay!"

"Pa has a meeting at seven," I told Charlie, when he'd gone. "But boy, I'm glad he came up here!"

"Yeah," Charlie said. "It sure was keen of him. I mean, when he's not one bit interested."

I kind of gasped.

"You know what I mean," Charlie said. "He's—the coach."

"Right," I said. And I was just a flop. Pa hadn't felt any muscles.

That night I had to walk my bike home from Mr. Kirby's. I was tired. I went right to bed and to sleep. But all of a sudden I woke up and sat up straight in the dark. I could hear Ma saying, *"I hope Francie feels all right for her birthday tomorrow!"*

That was what Mom had been saying when Dad and I came upstairs. I had a chill. It was one A.M. and it was Francie's birthday. I hadn't gotten her a gift, and I didn't have one penny to buy one!

They say you can figure things out in your sleep, but I didn't take chances. I got up and pulled out my bottom dresser drawer and dug out the gift paper from the last book Kris gave me, *The Life and Times of Shakespeare*. The blue ribbon was there, too.

Next I wiped my transformer on my sheet—way down, where smudges don't matter. Then, feeling very sad-hearted, I wrapped up my transformer and tied the blue bow and put it on my dresser and went to bed.

When I went down to breakfast they were all waiting for Francie, so they could sing "Happy Birthday!" I put my gift with the others piled beside her plate.

"I hear Francie!" Mother smiled. She hummed a very soft "Do!" Dad puffed out his chest, and I puffed mine, and we saw one blue feather slipper on the stairs and one bare foot and then the blue shirttail and then Francie. Her blonde hair was flopping. She really did look like a princess, if you overlooked a few things.

Dad boomed out "Happy birthday to you!" and we all sang. I thought my voice seemed a little deeper than last time, more like Dad's.

Francie drifted to the table. She can drift, even when one foot is naked.

Ma brought that special egg dish that nobody but Francie likes.

"Open your gifts!" Jill said. "Go ahead!"

Francie was very quiet. She opened a real elegant rose-colored shirttail from Dad and rose slippers to match from Ma. There was a wallet from Kris and Jill.

"I wanted to get you *The Life of Samuel Johnson*," Kris said. "But Jill thought you'd like the wallet."

"Oh, I do. Thank you," Francie murmured. She sounded tired. Her traumatic experience must have been very traumatic, I thought.

She opened more little packages, and Kris pointed. "There's one more!"

76

"Yes." Francie picked up my package and undid it with a thumb and one finger, and picked out the transformer the same way.

"It's a transformer," I said. "A very good one! It cost three dollars, Francie! Three dollars, when the snow comes."

Francie stared at it and began to bawl. "Oh, boo-hoo! Boo-hoo! I've got the terriblest family in the world!" She pointed at me. "Do you know what that terrible boy did?"

I gasped and squirmed. Francie was sure off my list of people who liked me!

Dad cleared his throat. "I would say he gave you something very precious to him."

"Out of a junk heap! And what will Harve think?" Francie wailed. "And Harve's mother!"

"Honey." Ma put her hand over Francie's. "We know you have a headache, but we've all tried—"

"Who wouldn't have a headache?" Francie howled. "Do you know what happened to me? Harve walked me home from school yesterday! The first day Daddy has let him have a minute to breathe! So we walked down Garfield Street to avoid Dot Speaker and the kids. And what do you suppose this nausical boy did?"

"I'm innocent!" I said, and there was the funniest sound from Ma.

"It's not nausical," Kris said. "It's—" Kris wouldn't say it.

Francie went right on. "Mr. Anderley had all this unsightly garbage piled in front of his house. And just who do you suppose was going through it, picking out horrible objects and wiping his hands on his pants? Just as if the Cranes are trash pickers? And who do you suppose, if he's West Comet High's best athlete, is going to stoop to be seen with a trash picker's sister, whose only brother is a trash picker?"

My face felt hot. All the guys pick trash to get stuff for their rigs. I wished I knew how to make her understand.

There were about six expressions on Dad's face. Mom looked as if she was holding back a laugh and would hold it back if she burst.

Jill was mad. "Now look, Frances Crane—" But Francie was bawling into her sleeve so loud she didn't hear.

Dad made for the door, coughing, and trying to say, "I'm late!" Mom hurried behind him, to get kissed good-bye.

"I'll find your other slipper, Francie," Kris said.

Jill picked up the transformer and handed it to me.

I took it to my room and wrote a note. *"Dear Francie: I will do the dishes for a week. Happy Birthday! E.C."*

I helped Kris make Francie's bed. Then I put the note on her pillow.

Well, this was no morning to start explaining that I needed Christmas and birthday money for my transmitter. But Jill would plug for it, and I had high hopes.

I wasn't worried about money to buy gifts. We have this Christmas club and part of our allowance goes in it each week. So that was OK.

Dad's team won the Marshton game and cinched

the conference championship. The market was up. Of course it would be down again. Basketball was looming. But at the moment the West Comet Comets were the champs. I felt pretty cheerful.

Then it happened. It was Saturday morning. Ma was putting up decorations and humming her solo for the Christmas choir concert, when Webber came over.

He had a package in his hand—in his glove, I mean. He didn't have a jacket, but he had on gloves to keep his violin fingers warm.

"Mrs. Crane," he said, "Mother sent some fruitcake and said to ask you if the hickory tree has to look that way all through the Christmas season, as it doesn't harmonize with our outdoor decorations." All this time he was looking up the stairs.

Ma came down from her ladder, smiling. "Well, thank you for the fruitcake, Webber. As for the hickory tree, it's old and tough and it does have to stay there, so—"

"Mother!" Kristan wailed. "You *know* Webber means Eric's antenna!"

Ma smiled at Webber. "So I'll pack you some Christmas cookies, dear. Meanwhile, why don't you run up and see how Eric's coming along?"

Webber didn't even hear the last. He was on his way upstairs. Ma went to the phone. I heard her saying, "Mattie, we can hide that tree so you won't have to see it at all! We have this tremendous red Santa in his sleigh, and I can get Andy to fasten it up in the tree and turn it toward your house. . . . Why, of course it's artistic! Little Gordy Adkins made it for Scouts. . . .

Mattie, it's true I didn't finish my painting, but I know art! . . . Well . . . Well, then, if you really don't mind the antenna. . . . Thank you for the fruitcake, Mattie, dear. Look for Webber to bring you some cookies!"

She didn't need to look for the cookies right away. With the new antenna, I could get more stations in daytime. Webber was fascinated. He listened, and listened, and listened—without earphones.

"My uncle is a ham," he said. "I saw his outfit when we visited there, but I guess I was too little to be interested."

After Webber left, Kris buzzed around me like a hornet. "How can you take Webber through that terrible room and past that terrible patchwork quilt, with all that unsightly junk on it?"

"Look," I said. "You know I'm between bedspreads."

I should have been prepared. I guess I'm dumb. And the last days before Christmas were so happy. I mean, we were out of school. The snow came. I got my transformer paid for. I paid all my debts.

Everybody was out and in with packages. The kitchen smelled wonderful. Francie was sweet to everyone because Harve had a little skip between football and basketball. I was just full of Ho! Ho! Ho!

It seemed to me that I could see a beautiful transmitter sitting right there in my shack. I was *so* sure, that when they handed me my big present Christmas eve I *knew* they had actually bought a rig, with Charlie's help and advice.

It was in a box, because it was very special. *Sculptured*, they said.

"You've wanted it a long time. You've been so patient," Ma said.

And Kristan said, "It's your Christmas *and* birthday gift. It's simply beautiful, Eric! The most beautiful in all this town! You'll be proud to take—*anyone*—upstairs to see it!"

"Thanks," I said, in a funny, funny voice.

Because my big gift was a sort of cream-colored bedspread, and I was almost bawling.

And so was Jill.

I Have Just One Year

Basketball is much worse than football. "I've got to produce," Dad said. "We impressed nobody last year."

"Andrew Crane," Ma said, "your teams are the only reason West Comet is ever heard of! The Comets are the champions!"

"And their coach's wife *could* be prejudiced!" Dad said. "Smack!" That was a kiss. "The Comets *were* the champs, honey. That was football. This is basketball."

Anyone can see why I was right on my own, getting a transmitter.

"You'll get it, Eric," Mr. Kirby encouraged.

Mr. Painter, at school, did not. "Eric," he said in class one day, "if your mind's on a problem, it's not the one at hand. If you don't knuckle down, you'll carry home a C!"

I shivered. "I'll knuckle down." No Crane ever got a C.

Meanwhile, I was studying like mad for my exam for my novice class license. So were Charlie and Don and Bill, and Hank Thomas and Mike Miller.

"But if I do pass, I can't go on the air without a transmitter," I told Jill and Betsy.

Betsy almost cried. Her eyelashes had tears on them. She's the funniest girl. You can't hate her. "I'm saving, Eric," she said.

"I'll get along. But thanks, Betsy." She *is* the best Burnside.

"I'm saving, too," Jill said.

So was I. Scrounging and saving. There was lots of snow and I am a good shoveler. I had one trouble. My jobs seemed to be across town from each other. But I travel fast on foot. And I had to.

"You're all sending and copying five words a minute," Mr. Kirby said one night. "I think we'd better write for your exam papers."

On a Thursday afternoon Francie met me at the door. She fluttered an envelope with the FCC return address at me and began to cry.

"Eric, it says 'Official Business'! You've been drafted!"

While I wondered if I could put her on my list of people who like me, Kris came. She was brisk. "Francie, how ignorant can you be?" Then she stared at some school papers in my hand. "Eric Crane, did some teacher have to send Mother a note?"

"Miss Jones threw at me," I said, and ran upstairs. I made one stop to pick up some of Francie's underwear and drop it down the chute. Then I shut myself in my shack.

In no time, Ma was there. "Eric, what did Miss Jones throw at you, and why?"

I grinned. "Only a theme, Ma. When I answered Kris, I just left out a couple words. You know how that bugs her."

Ma shook her head. "I'm afraid you're still getting even for the bedspread. Kris was very sincere."

"Oh, fine!" I tapped the FCC envelope. "Ma, this is from the Federal Communications Commission. It contains my exam for my novice class amateur radio license. If I pass, I'll be a novice amateur radio operator, without anything to operate. But with a sincere sister, and a very fine bedspread—in my dresser! That helps a lot!"

Ma sighed and looked around. I was using my bed for a worktable. I had a pillow and a few blankets on the floor.

"Honey," Ma said gently, "the Meverden game is coming up."

Ma always dreads the Meverden game. It means a long bus trip. It's ninety miles—the farthest the team goes.

"Don't worry," I said. "I won't bother Dad. The other fellows have to scrounge and trade, too. I have to run now before the post office closes. I want to make my appointment with Mr. Kirby to give me my test. CUL!"

"CUL!" Ma said. See you later! Ma's great.

I took my test alone. Mr. Kirby gave me a five-words-per-minute code test. He used my set, because I was used to it. I got twenty-five words of about five letters each. I had to copy twenty-five consecutive letters that he sent. I had to send for a minute, at five words per minute.

Then Mr. Kirby opened the written exam and watched me take it. It was a multiple choice test and not too bad. Mr. Kirby signed, sealed, and mailed it.

Mr. Kirby did the same for all the guys. Then we had to wait.

There was plenty to think about while I waited. Dad's team lost a game. The *Clarion* boxed a column in black: *Crepe hangs all over the mourning bench in West Comet High gym. The dirge sounds. Enter the chief mourner, Andy Crane. . . .*

At home the market was below visible level. Francie couldn't go to any more games. "You jinx them," Dad said.

At school Mr. Painter was feeling better, but Miss Jones called me in about a theme. "It just isn't up to the family standard, Eric. It doesn't count much toward your period grade, but the next one—"

"I'll do better! What's the next theme about, Miss Jones?"

"You'll choose your subject."

"I'll write about building a transmitter!" I told her.

I had my transformer and some tubes. I scrounged a tuning condenser from an old radio Mr. Peterman gave me. The guys ordered crystals, but they had to send money with the order. I hadn't sent for mine.

We wound our own coils and saved money. We traded around for things like tube sockets, capacitors, resistors. Older hams gave us things. Don Bishop's mother saves bottle caps. She gave us beauties, to make knobs. I got a set of gold ones.

I had some of my work done, when my license came. Jill was standing there holding her breath, with her eyes as big as moons.

"I passed!" I told her. "See!" I showed her my license with my call letters—WN9JEF. She whooped and ran to tell Betsy.

I did no whooping. I put the license in my wallet and looked at it thoughtfully. The N was for Novice. The license couldn't be renewed. I could transmit code on a low power transmitter for one year. Then I had to pass the general class exam, or I was washed up.

I had just one year—and my transmitter wasn't finished!

But all the guys passed, and was Mr. Kirby tickled! "Excuse me if I strut a little!" he said. "It's always a thrill, since the day George Peterman passed!" Mr. Peterman was the first ham Mr. Kirby ever helped, and Mr. Peterman has a little bald spot, now.

We were all in Mr. Kirby's shack so he phoned the *Clarion* and Marty Speaker came right over with his camera. Marty is a poor guy who has Dot Speaker, who is Francie's best friend, for a sister.

Marty took a fine picture. It was on Page Seven, right next to the Symphonette Concert news. Charlie was sitting at Mr. Kirby's rig, wearing phones and looking important. The rest of us were hovering around him, grinning.

Mr. Kirby beamed. "Wait till your dad sees this, Eric!"

But there was another picture in the *Clarion*—on the sports page. It was Coach Durbin, over at Junior High, with his basketball team—the team I would be on, if I were not a flop and a failure.

Dad looked at it a long time. He said, "I hope they'll have a lot of flit, when they come to me!" He smiled at me. "Mother says you're in the paper, too."

"Page Seven," I said.

"Oh! The other part!"

Of course. The other part. The no-good part. Not the sports page. But Dad kept nodding. "Congratulations! Real fine, Eric!"

Real, real third-rate, he meant. I knew. It just took the joy out of everything when I thought about his great disappointment in me.

Supper was quiet. I, for one, was thinking about my problems. Ma said, "Mrs. Burnside has a new idea. She thinks if we could get the Mayhew house for a Woman's Club and Art Center we could really have some culture in West Comet."

"She can't get it," Dad said.

And I said, "Please excuse me."

Later, I listed my needs and resources. I needed some sheet aluminum and a meter from Mean John. I needed QSL cards. I still hadn't ordered my crystal. The resources list was short—seventy-five cents.

I glanced in my mirror. Desperate—as usual.

So—I took the paper route.

There aren't too many paper routes in West Comet. Ralph Coleman gave his up to take a supermarket job. He told me at noon, so after school I hustled down to the *Clarion* and got the route and carried it that very day.

When I got home Kris sniffed my paper bag. "What's *that?*"

"I took a *Clarion* route," I said.

Francie gasped, but Kris spoke first. "Who had that bag last? Has it been sterilized?"

"Ralph Coleman had it."

Kris screamed. "His sister had mononucleosis!"

I grinned. "Yeah. The bag was full of monnycoddles. I shook 'em all out, though. You can look."

Francie was glaring at me. She had on her old blue shirttail and a blue slipper and a rose one. "Just where is your route?"

"It starts on Yale. It takes in Denis and Third and Gray—"

"I knew it!" Francie wailed. "What will Mrs. Bonner think when my own brother comes peddling her paper and calling for sixty cents at the back door on Saturday? Mother, two of Harve's uncles are Harvard professors!"

"Eric is too young to be a Harvard professor," Ma said. "And, Kris, the bag looks clean to me."

Jill was standing there. She had a new haircut that Kris gave her. Her bangs were real straight across her forehead and her hair was shiny and smooth right to her shoulders, where it turned up just a little. Her face is about the cleanest face you see. But she was mad.

"Francie," she said, "the cleaner can't get the big pop stain out of your new rose shirttail unless you will absolve him of all blame if it makes a hole. Also—" she pointed—"there's chocolate on your face, and both those slippers are for your right foot. And—"

While she was talking, I made it upstairs. I don't know what I'd do without Jill!

She came up later with some money. "For your crystal, Eric. Some is from Francie, because she was proud of your picture in the paper, which will impress Harve's mother."

I put Francie on my list. Not on the top, but almost. "I'll pay you both, next snowstorm," I said. "I can get my QSL cards printed, too. Thanks—Butch."

She loves that. She glowed. "Ask Daddy for the metal and meter, Eric. *I'll* ask him!"

Friday, Dad's team won the regional title in a tough overtime game. "The worst game we ever played!" he said. "Absolutely the worst!"

The next week he dropped the second game of the sectional, and the market hit *dirge*. I sold my skates, and Jill sold Kris my book called *Stories of Ten Great Operas* which Aunt Isabel gave me, because Kris told her I was quite ignorant about opera.

So I went down to Mean John's. He was in his back rooms, playing his violin like mad. He came out and scowled at me. When he's been playing and hears that bell he always looks like someone trying to wake up from some dream that he liked better than the shop.

"You!" he said. There was a five-hundred-page book in that one word.

"Yes, sir," I said. "Mr. Spencer—"

"I know. You have only a year. If you don't get some sheet aluminum you'll die, and my business will fold up, of course."

"Sir, I'll need enough for my chassis and panel—"

"I *know!* You smart alecks tell me everything—except how you're going to pay for your junk!"

"I'll pay with money, sir."

"How—revolutionary! Next snowstorm? Next *Clarion* payday?"

"Today, sir."

"Stop gabbing!" he growled. "Can't you see I'm busy?"

He cut the metal and I just stared because he could do such perfect work. "This is the panel." He held up a piece. "You'll be bending it, so. And when you make your openings, watch it. If you do a botched job, don't come whining around me."

"Sir," I said, "would you have a meter? It has a jewel movement—"

"I *know* that!" he barked. "I don't need sprouts like you telling me what kind of movement a meter has!"

"Yes, sir." I gave him my money. He held it and looked at me.

"Tha-" I choked. I had almost thanked him, which would be a grave social error. I bolted for the door.

"Come back, you!" Mean John yelled. He was waving two dollars at me. "Come back and get your change! If you think I'm going through the snow with it tonight, like Abraham Lincoln—"

"But—you said eight dollars!"

"I said six!" he barked. "And get out of here, before I crack something over your head!"

I got. I had made a very successful visit. I had not thanked him. I had not hurt him.

Mrs. Burnside came over after supper to cheer Dad up. Dad was out of sight, so she cheered Ma. "Hilda, this year we're going to have more culture in West Comet, if it kills me! The Ingeborgs are going to have more entries in the tri-county art exhibit. Then, we're doing more about music. We do have Symphonette, and a concertmaster who has been on the concert stage, besides being the sweetest man in this town. I think we should import one really famous guest singer!"

The sweetest man. *Mean John! Jeepers!* "Kris," I whispered, "wait till the sweetest man busts something over Webber's head!"

Kris didn't hear me. She was hoping Mrs. Burnside would say something about darling Webber—and she did. "We must have more opportunities! Artistic youth, like Webber, must not be starved! I spoke to Eldred again about the Mayhew house. If we could even *rent* it—"

Eldred is Mr. Burnside, the banker. He is very seldom mentioned.

"Who owns it, Mattie?" Ma asked. "Maybe Andrew could try—"

"If Eldred W. Burnside knows who owns it, he won't tell me," Mrs. Burnside said. "He says it's owned by someone in New York."

"The place is kept up. Eldred must know who pays the taxes."

"He insists he doesn't. The owner's lawyers deal with him."

There Mrs. Burnside noticed me and paused to do a little reforming. "Eric, I thought hamming kept boys at home."

"Just off the street, Mattie," Mom smiled.

I said, "I just go to hams' houses. I was home last night."

"I know," Mrs. Burnside said. "You left your light on all night, dear."

I smiled. "I was up most of the night. Miss Jones

passed out in English class and I thought I'd better do something about it."

I bolted for the stairs, but Ma got my ear. "You apologize, young man! You explain to Mrs. Burnside!"

I said, "Well, Mrs. Burnside, sometimes I talk so fast that I leave out a word. Miss Jones passed out some questionnaires and wanted them back. Ouch, Ma!"

Mrs. Burnside was nodding, fast. "I see. I see. Hilda, his ear is getting red! I knew he was joking! I have a boy!"

Pa came in, then. One glance told me the track team was not shaping up, and Harve Bonner's head was on crooked, and the market was down.

I was glad I could make my own transmitter.

I was very thankful for the paper route.

A Ham Is Badly Shaken

Track season is worse than basketball. Dad came home from clocking runners to sweat over statistics. "Even West Comet has some records to live up to," he told us at dinner.

"Yes," Mom said. "Yours."

"Don't speak of mine!" Dad barked. "Not after the basketball tourney!"

I love that guy when he barks. I looked in the buffet mirror and wondered if my jaw was getting sterner and my eyes a little steelier and my jaws a little more rugged, like his.

"Honey," Ma said, "you reached the second game of the sectional and had two good players out with flu."

"Thanks," Pa said, "for the only kind words I've heard from an innocent bystander."

This was a slight exaggeration. I've noticed the *Clarion* kids the tragic coach when he's winning, or when he drops a minor one, but if he loses a big one there are no cracks. After the sectionals there was only praise for a great coach, a valiant team.

"Next year has to be my year," Pa said. "Time *is*. Next year, or never!" I felt him looking at me. "Where you been, Skipper?"

Francie answered for me. "Eric Crane disgraced us! He took a paper route!" She shook too much salt on her chop and stared at it. She was off my list.

"OK, Princess. I'm earning four bucks a week, and I need it!" I said. "Dad, I've got a year! Just a—wait!" I counted. "Time goes fast. I've got about ten months to get ready for my general class exam. So I carry my paper route and hurry home. I really have to sprint, if my bike's laid up. I do my assignments. Then I study theory or work at my rig. I have to learn to send and copy thirteen words a minute."

Jill pulled at Dad's sleeve. "Daddy, Eric has contacted a ham in Nebraska!"

"I think it was Nebraska," I said. "I lost him in the QRM."

"QRM is general interference," Jill said. She gave me a smile. "But—just think! Nebraska! Eric just sat there and communicated—free!"

"Not by voice," I explained. "It's code, while I'm a novice." I reached in my wallet and put a QSL card down in front of Dad. It was printed in blue, and looked keen. "For you," I said. "And I have to ask your XYL to excuse me. I have a SKED."

Kris was shocked. "Mother, that sort of talk at your dinner table is demoralizing! It was probably you whom he was calling an XYL."

I gave Mom a QSL card. "XYL is ham for wife," I explained. "It's OK. It only means ex-young lady."

"And exactly what," Kris demanded, "is a SKED?"

"A—a date!" I said. "CUL!" I made for the stairs.

"Does he *mean* that?" I heard Francie breathe. "Is he at last growing up? That boy has absolutely no social life! If he ever gets to Harvard, no fraternity will have him! Mother, next year his class will have some parties, and we'll simply have to insist—"

I only wished I had a SKED. That's an agreement to contact another ham at a specified time. I tuned up and began to call: CQ CQ CQ DE WN9JEF WN9JEF WN9JEF. I was pretty slow and I knew no one but a beginner would care to work me.

I called for a full minute and tapped a K and stood by, hoping for an answer from Paris, France, although I would settle for one from the next street.

That was what I got. After several calls I heard my own letters coming back to me. WN9JEF WN9JEF WN9JEF DE WN9JDG WN9JDG WN9JDG. Wot say OM?

It was only Charlie, but was I tickled! I answered him. WN9JDG WN9JDG WN9JDG DE WN9JEF WN9JEF WN9JEF. TNX OM BT BT BT.

We entertained each other a while. Pretty slow, but good practice. At nine we signed off, and put our entries in our log books.

I tuned around, looking for other contacts. I was not very successful, although I contacted K9BBT—Rhinie Bauer, in Meverden. He was at the mike of his dad's battery set.

Two nights later, at eleven o'clock, Kris rapped on my door and opened it. "Didn't you see the new sign?" I asked her.

RADIO STATION WN9JEF
ON THE AIR!
SILENCE!

"Oh, I thought that was for drips," Kris said. "Eric, I hope you've done your homework. Because if you bring home one failing grade you have to give up that outfit!"

"Who said so?"

"D-Daddy said so!" She closed the door.

I wondered when. Because I had read the *Clarion*.

"Turtles I've got," Coach Andy Crane told us, with customary tragedy in every line of his face, when we stopped over at the athletic field behind the West Comet High Halls of Learning, to see how the track team is coming along. "I've got runners who stop and gossip with girls or polish their fingernails as they jog along," the melancholy coach continued. "As for jumpers, any self-respecting Mexican jumping bean will clear the bars they bump their heads on! I've got puny, short-legged little mudders. . . ."

Confidentially, dear readers, Andy was deliberately coloring it blue. This reporter feels a few of those turtles and mudders must have been on stilts. We would have asked them, if they had been willing to bend down to our five-feet-eleven level for a little conversation. And while their coach wiped copious tears on his sopping sleeve, this reporter also got an eye on the stopwatch and it seemed to him that a few runners managed to get there—like flying low. And among the jumpers, not one came to have a bumped heady kissed. . . .

On and on. I guessed Dad was too busy to think about my grades. But I pulled switches and went to bed.

Saturday evening Charlie and Don came over. I

made three contacts—all local. Not exactly showing off. One was Rhinie Bauer again.

At nine I called once more. CQ CQ CQ WN9JEF WN9JEF WN9JEF. When I hit the K and stood by the first time, I got an answer. If I remember, it was something like WN4AYN. Anyway, we looked him up in Charlie's call book and the ham was in Florida. *Florida!*

We had snow that night. He said it was 78 down there. He was glad to work me. He used to live in Meverden, and he used to play basketball. He had heard we had a tough coach in West Comet. He wanted us to say hello to two people. He could really pound the brass, but we all copied, so we got the message before he signed off.

The fellows watched me post my log book. They were excited. "You'll get a QSL from Florida, Eric!" Don smacked. "Mr. Kirby will think that's something!" He added politely, "Your dad will, too, of course."

"Yeah!" I grinned. "Say—I'm hungry!"

"Me, too!" Charlie said. "I didn't know it was ten o'clock!"

"Wait!" Don corrected him. "It's twenty-two zero zero!"

"And I didn't eat since—twelve zero zero," I said. "I forgot supper. Let's go down. I think I smelled a cake."

It was twenty-four little cakes. They were oblong, and they had fancy frosting on them, with little colored flowers. I bit one. "It's good. Some kind of chocolate," I said. "I'll get the milk."

That's one thing about hamming. You do forget supper and have to pick up what you can find in the night.

We were real hungry. But the last time I passed the cakes, the guys refused.

"There are six in your family," Charlie said. "We ought to leave one for everybody." Hams are thoughtful.

So the fellows left, and I was in bed when I remembered the English theme. It had to be turned in Friday. "Without *fail*," Miss Jones had said, looking right at me, although Charlie said it was at him.

I got up and went to my desk. I knew all about building my transmitter, but knowing something and knowing how to write it down are two different things.

I was slaving on it when Kris came in. "Eric," she said, "your light glares right in Webber's window. He'll have a headache tomorrow."

"Pull the shades," I said, "and he'll have a headache tonight. From eyestrain. Those shades are hard to see through."

If Webber saw her, Kris looked OK. She had two little braids, with a black bow on the end of each. She had on orange and black pajamas and black slippers, and, believe me, each slipper was on the foot it was made for. She pulled the shades and came to look at my theme.

"When is that due?"

"Day after tomorrow," I moaned.

"That's just ducky! Where's your bedspread?"

I kept my dignity. "I've been in bed. I certainly don't sleep under that expensive sculptured Christmas present."

Suddenly Kris went away. In a minute she was back with a dust mop. "I'll dig you out."

"Now, Kris!" I said. "Jeepers! It's twenty-three zero zero!"

"Twenty-three zero zero?"

"Eleven o'clock."

She blinked. "So what? I'm wide awake. So are you. So—"

I don't know anyone else like Kris, and I don't know whether I'm glad or sorry. My room sparkled when she got through.

"How's the theme?" she said.

I moaned again.

"Well, there's tomorrow. Come straight home from the paper route and stay away from the rig. If you flunk, you'll stay away from it quite a while, remember! It's twenty-three zero zero!" She clapped her hands. "Go on! To bed! Time is!"

Time was. I was almost asleep. In bed, I had a funny, safe feeling. A feeling that Kris wouldn't let me flunk. A feeling that Kris was on my list of people who like me.

When I woke up it was morning and somebody awful mad was shaking me half out of my skin. "I'll show you!" Shake! Shake! "I'll teach you! You miserable, sneaky little horse thief!" Shake! Shake! My teeth rattled. "You little fox! You sneaky little red-headed fox in a chicken coop!" Shake! Shake!

I managed to get one eye to focus and saw that it was Kris. She was so mad that she was crying, and Kris doesn't cry.

"Get out of that bed, because I'm going to pulverize you, if it's the last thing I do!" Shake! Shake!

Shaking a dust mop sure makes muscles! Mighty me!

"What the—Kris! You gone off your rocker?"

"Watch—your—grammar!" She got my collar. Shake! Shake! "I'll boost you down those stairs so fast you'll think a tornado struck you, and you can explain to Dad!"

"Now, Kris! Get hold of yourself! You must be imagining something!"

"Hah! I *imagine* I left twenty-four—*twenty-four*—beautiful French pastries in the cupboard for my Latin Club party. Twenty-four French pastries that I had slaved over! And you and those other horse thieves went sneaking down in the night and gobbled them up, and—" Shake! "And—left—crumbs—all—over—the—floor!"

"Kris, I didn't *know*—"

"Ignorance is not innocence! If it were, you'd be a saint!" She reached to grab me again, but instead she wheeled around and ran out.

I took her off my list of people who like me.

I got dressed and went to her door. Kris was in her little pink chair with her head on the arm.

"Kris?" I said. "Kris, you're a wonderful cook! Even if they were French, they were awful good!"

That did it. Up came her face. "Get *out!*" she screamed.

I went downstairs and she came behind me, crying. Ma and Francie and Jill were standing at the foot of the stairs like a receiving line at a wedding, except that their eyes were popping and their mouths were open.

"Kristan, Eric didn't *know!*" Jill said.

Mom put her arm around Kris. "Honey, there are thousands of French pastries in the world, but only one Eric Crane, who's your brother."

"Thank heaven!" Kris pulled away from Mom. "Where's Father?"

Father! We absolutely never call Pa "Father" except in tragic cases of extreme emergency.

"Kris!" Francie grabbed her. "The track meets are beginning! You *wouldn't!*"

"Oh, *wouldn't* I?" Kristan's voice trembled. *"Webber* belongs to the Latin Club!"

Right then we heard the car back down the drive. Boy, was I relieved! "Ma," I said, "I've often seen cakes like those at Kanes'."

"Do you know what they cost?" Kris demanded. "For your information, they're a quarter! Twenty-five cents apiece!" She wiped her eyes and glared at me. "Also," she said, "it's 'very good,' not 'awful' or 'terrible' good! Even a horse thief should describe the objects he steals in good English!"

"Ma," I said, "if you'll loan me the money for the cakes I'll go without my allowance until it's all paid back."

"I have a better idea," Ma said. "Everyone come to breakfast, and—Oh, dear! Here comes Mattie! Kris—"

"I'll be a lady, Mother," Kris said.

"Listen, everyone!" Mom whispered. "We'll have peanut butter sandwiches for lunch! And I'll have French pastries at school at 3:30. —Oh, good morning, Mattie!" She gave Mrs. Burnside a dazzling smile.

"What do you suppose? Kris just found out she needs French pastries for Latin Club at 3:30! So I have my day cut out for me!"

"I'll help you," Mrs. Burnside said. "Kristan—" She patted her. "I'm glad you don't settle for ordinary cupcakes. I've got a new, fine pastry tube that will put the most exquisite rosebuds on the cakes. I'll go home and give Webber and Betsy breakfast and be right back!"

She would have to pry old Webber out of bed first, I knew. Off she bustled. I still felt shook up, but I grinned. Mrs. Burnside had tried to reform me for many little bits of evildoing. This morning I was very evil. I was a sneaky horse thief, and she didn't even suspect! She had missed her biggest chance.

But that night she sent Webber over. Although I wasn't delighted, I couldn't help noticing Webber was beginning to look like more of a guy. He had a shorter haircut, and he was getting thinner. He gave us all a grin, and oh, man, did Kristan smile back!

"I hate to bother," Webber said, "but somebody's going to conduct a TV art tour—"

"Oh, yes!" Ma said. "I know about it, Webber. I'll be watching."

"Well," Webber said, "I hope you won't think this is my idea. But we've been getting some interference on our TV and Mother's worried." Here, Webber actually winked. "You know Mother. She thinks the interference comes from your rig, Eric. She wondered if you could leave it off that night."

"He certainly can!" Kris said. "Can't you, Eric?"

"I don't think the interference is from me," I said.

"But the TV repairman will put a filter on your set and there won't be any interference in the future. It doesn't cost much."

"Never thought of that!" Webber said. "Say! I'll see to it!" He looked at the stairs. "That radio sure keeps you busy, doesn't it, Eric?"

I wanted to say, "You, too, doesn't it?" But I said, "Ya. Like to go up a while?"

"Sure! I've got time!"

He had time, all right. I had intended to work on my theme, but a crowbar wouldn't have jogged Webber loose. The guy was absolutely fascinated by the QSL cards on my wall and by my log book entries— especially that one honey—Florida.

He stayed and stayed. Once I heard Kris in my room and smelled fresh perfume. This was strange for Kris does not waste perfume. After a while I heard her typewriter going like mad.

It was half past nine when Webber remembered his homework. Kris came downstairs behind us, calling, "Anybody else hungry?"

"Yes, thank you," Webber said.

"I am!" I said.

So we went to the kitchen, and believe it or not Kris came up with the six French pastries we guys had saved.

Now, there is a funny thing about me. With me, enough is enough. I had eaten six of those pastries last night, and had been beaten up for it in the morning, and I just couldn't look at them.

"I'll have a jelly sandwich," I said.

While Kris was coaxing Webber to have the last

pastry, I remembered. "Jeeps! My theme! Excuse me!" I made for the stairs.

Two things were on my desk. One was the book, *Stories of Ten Great Operas*. The other was my theme, all typed up, with a note on it.

Dear Eric: This is a good theme, but some corrections had to be made. Copy it tonight, and in the morning I will talk to you about the changes I made in spelling and punctuation, etc., so you won't make the same mistakes again. Love, Kris.

I put Kris back on my list of people who like me, and sat down and began to copy my theme.

A Journey With a Posthole Digger

Track was over. West Comet High had set three new records. School was out at last. Some people had vacation, but I had to stay in town to keep my paper route.

Francie got a summer car-hop job, and Kris was an assistant camp counselor. Jill went to camp, but she was home most of the summer.

Pa had some programs, but he set aside some time to build me up for Coach Durbin's team. I did my best. I listened to all he said, and I tried to remember. I ate. I exercised to build muscle. I grew two inches, got a tan, and looked more rugged.

Pa worked me out quite often. I kicked. I tackled. I ran, although I was usually tuckered from my other running. It seemed as if I ran all summer. My bike always gave out at the wrong end of town, five minutes before I had to be at the other end, and I'd have to leg it as fast as I could.

There were a few good things. Mr. Kirby was taking his vacation in the fall, and most of the fellows were in town, so we kept right on meeting at his house and he gave us workouts, too.

The best thing was that Webber went to music camp, and Mrs. Burnside hardly touched base at home. She was at this conference and that and off painting pictures. Of course she did not neglect the Cranes. She wrote Ma letters from everywhere and begged her to get her painting going for fall. But she did not come home to reform me, and I could sit at my rig all night if I wanted to. I got lots of time to practice my code and study for my written exam. All the fellows were busy getting ready.

In September Ma bought me some longer pants and bigger shirts and jackets and socks and Sunday shoes, and Dad said, "You report for football, Skipper. You should make it!"

Mr. Kirby said, "You can soon apply for your exam. I know you can make it."

Well, Pa was wrong. I tried. I did my best, but I just was not like the guys on the team. I told Dad myself. His face was kind of stony, and I wished I was dead. I hoped it wasn't the last chance I'd ever have to make my dad proud of me.

"Dad," I said, "I'll be taking my general class exam in November. The guys are going to Chicago, and—"

"That's fine!" Dad said. "I know you've worked hard, Eric."

I tried again. "I—I'll have to go to Chicago, and—"

The phone was ringing for Dad, and I guess I was glad. Most of the guys had most of their money, but you don't up and ask your dad for twenty dollars at a time like this.

I decided I would wait for November, although I knew every week would be worse. Dad had a football conference championship to defend, and the market would always be down.

Test time got closer. Mr. Kirby drilled us hard. He

warned us about everything. We would have to send and copy thirteen words a minute, but he drilled us at fifteen. He told us the pitfalls.

"I want you to go to Chicago with your eyes wide open. You'll be examined in a strange place. Strangers will run the test. We could make timing errors at home. There, you'll have no hand sending. It will be thirteen words per minute on tape, and you'll have to be on your toes. You won't necessarily get intelligible sentences. You won't have much time to fill in. I want you to go prepared and to know exactly what you're facing. Then you won't get buck fever."

Well, I was prepared, except in the financial department. I decided to sell a few articles I didn't need. I typed up a list of things for sale and on Saturday morning when I went out collecting for the *Clarion* I handed each lady a list.

ERIC CRANE'S RESALES
GREAT VALUES

Rock Collection	**$4.00**
Fishbowl (fish food provided)	**.25**
Binoculars in case. I am fifth owner	**1.00**
3 sweat shirts, blue, yellow, gray.	
One is patched	**1.00**
Lamp shade, pink	**.20**
1 Bedspread, cream. Sculptured. Colonial.	
Never used	**8.00**
Big books	**.50**
Small books	**.10**
Picture in gold frame	**.25**
Chemistry set. Not used lately	**3.00**

Believe it or not, I sold everything except two big books and the rock collection. Every lady asked about the bedspread, and the lady who bought it was Harve Bonner's mother.

"Eric," she said, "does your mother know you're selling it?"

"Well, in a way, Mrs. Bonner," I said. "I asked Ma if she cared if I sell a few things which have not been used for a long time, because I'm cleaning out my room and don't wish to clutter the attic. And Mom said, 'Would to heaven Andrew Crane had some ideas like that! You have my full permission, Eric, and heartfelt good wishes!'"

"I'll pay you right now," Mrs. Bonner said. "Write my name right on your list, so you won't forget."

"I won't forget," I said. "I'll go right home and get the bedspread." Nobody was home right then.

That night Mrs. Adkins called up and said Gordy wanted the rock collection, but could pay only two dollars. So I had twenty-three dollars, which was more than I needed for the trip to Chicago.

Mr. Kirby went with us. He was driving to Chicago anyway, he said. We had all been there with our folks, or something, and this trip was strictly business.

When we got the code test nobody got buck fever. Everyone passed, thanks to Mr. Kirby. We were all invited to sit down to our written exam.

It was a long sit for Don Bishop and me. The other guys were through earlier, but we didn't have to hurry, and a guy who has failed his dad can't take a chance on a second failure.

After Don and I finished we looked around town a little, at electronics stuff and a few trains. But Mr. Kirby had to work the next day and we considered him. We got an early supper and we were home at eight o'clock, and the long wait began.

After an exam is over, you begin to worry and wonder if you really did so well. Sometimes I woke up in the night shivering after a dream that every fellow passed except me.

I had other worries, too. If I passed I would be a real ham. I could transmit by voice. I needed a mike, a modulation transformer and speech amplifier. I needed a connector or jack and assorted hardware. And a better antenna. Charlie was getting one, and some of the other guys.

"A good antenna is something you have to have," Charlie said.

"Of course," I said, "we're counting that we'll pass the exam."

"Yes." Charlie looked worried. "We're—counting chickens!"

But the day I saw the wonderful metal pole at Mean John's, I knew I might not ever have such a good chance again. I talked it over with myself.

If I passed, I would need the antenna. If I didn't pass, I would try again. If I flunked and flunked I would be a complete failure and it wouldn't matter what happened to me, but my survivors could always sell a good metal pole.

My last check from the *Clarion* was gone. The market was down at home. Dad was worried. He had lost his seniors. Of course, he loses them every year, but every fall it seems they were the best seniors he ever had, and he was already feeling bad because Harve Bonner was at last a senior. He had a curfew on Harve, so Sid Temple kept the telephone ringing.

It was no time to ask for money to buy a metal pole, and now that I was taller and bigger I was getting a funny feeling about borrowing from Jill, although I knew she hadn't changed at all, except that she looked prettier in some new clothes she had.

So Charlie and I looked around my room. It was pretty well cleaned out, but there was something that I didn't think I would need.

When a fellow has a new, shiny pair of shoes that are waiting around because he is too busy to wear them, it's a waste.

"Leather shrinks," Charlie said. "They might get too small."

"Dad paid for them, and he earns his money the hard way," I said.

Out of family loyalty, I packed the shoes in the box they came in and Charlie and I took them down to Mean John's.

"I'm going with you," Jill said. She was half crying.

"So am I," said Betsy.

It was kind of like a funeral. The girls stayed outside. Charlie went in with me. Mean John was sitting at his counter. He had some music in front of him, but he was not working and he didn't seem to see us for a while. He had a look I had seen on him before, as if he was thinking about something way back, something that puzzled or bothered or worried him. It was almost a sad look. It almost made a guy feel sorry for him.

We stood and waited and after a while I realized he was looking at the box. In a deadly tired voice he said, "Your Sunday shoes."

I wondered how he knew. "They are very good shoes, sir," I said. "They don't have one scuff! I've polished my school shoes for church."

He seemed to think and think. I felt hot and cold. All of a sudden he nodded. "The pole! That's it! I left it out in sight!"

"Is it—still here, sir?"

He did not answer. He got up, looking very, very tired. He took the box from my hands and put my name on it and limped down to put it in his case.

"Will the pole cost m-more, sir?" I asked him.

He said, "No. If it would, I wouldn't let you have it. Go around to the back, and make it snappy. I'd like to get this over."

He was making it easy for me. I wanted that pole more than anything in the world right then. Unless, of course, I could some way have made the football team.

Charlie and I came out smiling, but we didn't let Mean John see us smile. The girls were standing at the corner of the building, looking like scared squirrels.

"I'm getting it!" I told them. "Wait here. We're going around back."

But they followed us, and it was a good thing they did. Mean John had put the pole out among the packing boxes and had slammed the door. We found out that pole was heavy. It took the four of us to lug it

home, and it was all we could manage. We had to put it down four times to rest our arms.

When we got in sight of the house I wanted Betsy to quit.

"I'm no quitter," she said. "Besides, Mother isn't home." She thought a minute. "Wait!" She sprinted toward her house and in two minutes we got the surprise of our lives. She came back and Webber was with her. Webber! He had been doing some growing, too.

"Say!" he said. "I'll help with that! Why didn't you tell me?"

"Look," I said. "You'll hurt your violin fingers and your Ma will blame me."

"It won't hurt me at all," Webber said. He yelled, "Oh, Harve!"

I shook. Harve Bonner was coming along with Francie. He grinned at us. "Harve," Webber said, "help me give the kids a hand with this."

"Sure!" Harve said. "Where do you want it?"

Jill answered. "In our backyard."

The two bigger guys wouldn't let us help. They carried the pole to the backyard and laid it down. "New clothesline pole?" Harve asked.

Jill smiled like an angel. "They do make good strong ones," she said. "Thanks so much, Harve. Thank you, Webber!"

Webber rubbed his hands together and he and Harve stood and talked a minute and everyone scattered except Charlie and me.

"Eric," Charlie sighed, "you'll have to dig an awful deep hole."

"Just deep enough to bury myself," I grinned. "When Francie starts howling because we called Harve away from her, when he's on curfew anyway!"

I don't understand girls. Francie never howled at all. I carried my paper route and went to my rig and forgot supper. I didn't see her until Saturday lunch and her mind was on the game, or something.

Kris said, "I hope you're not going to leave that horrible pole across the backyard. Our yard looks messy enough—"

"Well, Kris," I said, "if it's in the way or anything, just toss it to one side. I won't object."

Jill giggled. And Mom said, "No word from the exam, Eric?"

"Not—yet." I began sweating. I broke into a sweat every time I thought of the exam.

"You'll pass." Mom smiled at me. "You can't fail after the way you worked."

The telephone rang and it was Mrs. Burnside for Ma. We heard Ma saying, "On a game day? Mattie, you know I never go anywhere—Oh! Oh, Mattie, you'll have to forgive me! I forgot! Of course!"

She came from the phone, looking half ashamed, and half amused. "The Ingeborgs are having a little meeting, and I forgot we asked Webber to play for us. I'll have to go."

"You certainly will!" Kris said. "Daddy can win the Sampson game without you!"

The phone rang again. Charlie. "Look, Eric. I know where you can get a posthole digger. It's out at Mark Bickford's uncle's farm, and Mr. Bickford said you can borrow it, as he won't be digging postholes at this time of the year."

I had been out to the farm lots of times. It's three miles out of town and the road is paved. "My bike's in order," I said. "Could we go this afternoon?"

"I can't go," Charlie said. "I've got to do some deliveries and sweep out the store."

"I'll go alone," I said.

Jill and Betsy were going to the game. "Aren't you going?" I asked Francie.

"No." She was wearing her rose shirttail which had cleaned without making a hole, and she seemed kind of thoughtful and quiet. "Harve thinks I'd bring good luck," she said, "but Daddy thinks I'd jinx it, and Daddy is the only one who's prerogatived to think. So I'll stay home and wash dishes."

Kris gasped, but what she said was, "Maybe I should attend the Ingeborgs. Maybe I'd bring Webber luck."

"Be funny!" Francie said. She went to the kitchen and looked at the dishes and I remembered that when she came back she had a very interesting expression.

Mrs. Bishop stopped to pick up Mrs. Burnside and Webber and then Ma. When they were gone Kris and Jill came downstairs all ready for the game, and that was when Francie fainted.

She said, "I'll get those dishes started." She was drifting toward the kitchen when suddenly she fell on the sofa in this faint.

I was scared. I had never seen anyone faint before. Kris and Jill were scared, too. "We have to put her head down," Kris said. "Help us, Eric."

So I helped, but I was shaking. Steady, boy, steady.

"Her face is pink," Jill said, after a while.

Francie opened her eyes. "Where am I?" she said.

"Right—right here on the sofa," I told her. "You fainted."

"Oh," she murmured. "Did I?" Her eyelids fluttered. "The last I remember was a voice, calling as if from some distant shore. 'Come! Come with us, Frances, and never toil again!' And I was trying to say, 'Nay. Nay, do not lure me. The dishes are my obligation. I do not shirk my obligations. . . .'" She smiled at us wanly. She said, "I love you all. I should abhor to leave you. Maybe a walk, and a good breath of terra firma—"

"I think you'd better lie down again," Kris said.

"But the dishes—"

"Jill and I will do the dishes. Are you warm enough?"

"I'll get a blanket," Jill said. She bounced upstairs and came down with a blanket and tucked it over Francie, up to her chin.

"Oh, thank you!" Francie said. "I'll be all right. Do, please, run on to the game!"

"We'll get the game on the radio," Kris said. She and Jill went to the kitchen and put on their aprons. Kris came to the door. "Francie," she said kindly, "terra firma means the earth."

"Thank you," Francie sighed. "I—knew it, in my mind."

"Francie," I said, "will you be all right, if I leave you?"

"Fine," she said. "My faithful sisters will attend me."

So I got my bike and started out. After my shaking

118

stopped I remembered Jill's saying, "Her face is pink," and a thought came to me that made me wonder.

I understood people get white when they faint. I didn't notice that Francie was white. I was right there to bet her face had been pink all the while. I was right there to bet the Princess had pulled a fast one on us peasants!

At the farm Mr. Bickford was real nice to me. He did look worried about the bike. "A posthole digger is an awkward thing, Eric. It won't be fun, carting it three miles on a bike. If I had my car—but Ma went into town to a meeting of the Ingeborgs. Young Burnside's going to play his fiddle."

"I'll make it, Mr. Bickford," I said.

It wasn't easy, the main reason being that I got a flat tire. Which meant I had to walk, and half carry the bike, and carry the posthole digger two and one-half miles.

And as I struggled on, I thought about my troubles, how I might not pass my test, and, if I didn't, I would wish I was dead. And if I did pass, I would need new QSL cards and those parts for my transmitter.

Also, there was the bedspread. Kris was bound to find out I had sold it. Sometimes I thought she knew now.

Also, I had another great big worry that only Jill knew, and I was dreading the day that Francie and Kristan would find out.

My class was going to have a party.

It was almost four o'clock when I reached Roger's Corner Service Station. Roger is a very good friend.

He patched the tire and pumped it up and said, "You look tuckered. I'd drive you home if I weren't alone. Care to wait?"

"I'll make it," I told him. "I've got to get home and peddle my paper route."

"Well," he said, "be careful. A house-moving truck is stalled across Front Street and the traffic is jammed up."

You wouldn't think traffic in West Comet could get jammed, but people go through West Comet to get from one town to another.

I got into the jam. I kept close to the curb. The cars were just crawling, and so was I because it was not simple to balance that posthole digger. It rocked, and I grabbed and hugged it and heard somebody say, "Oh, Eric, be careful!"

I looked up and Ma was right beside me in Mrs. Bishop's shiny car that was her twenty-fifth anniversary present. Mrs. Burnside was in it, too, and two other dressed-up ladies and, believe it or not, Francie!

There was lots of noise. I had to yell. "Where'd Francie come from?"

Francie looked the other way.

"Oh, she had to run down to shop for something," Mother said. "And Mrs. Bishop kindly picked her up."

"Well, that's keen!" I yelled. "That's kind! Because she shouldn't walk. Francie fainted after you left!"

"Fainted!" Ma said. "Frances, is that so?"

"I was just hungry," Francie said in a delicate voice. "I've had a chocolate malt, and I feel fine now."

She was mad, and I knew why. One of the other

dressed-up ladies was Harve's mother, Mrs. Bonner.

"How's the football game coming?" I yelled.

"Oh, dear!" Mrs. Bishop said, "I forgot to put the radio on! Hilda, why didn't you tell me?"

She put her car radio on and West Comet had just beat Sampson. Then we got out of the traffic, and the ladies zoomed ahead of me.

I knew Francie was off my list of people who like me!

The bike was through for the day. I put it with the digger in the garage and carried my paper route on the dead run, and got home before Dad did.

Francie pounced on me. "I was never so embarrassed in my life! To be riding with Harve's mother, and have my own brother trailing along beside the car on that broken-down bike, trying to balance that unsightly fertilizer spreader, which had dirt on it!"

"You wanted a breath of terra firma," Jill said. "That's what you said after you fainted."

Ma began to laugh. She laughed so hard she cried.

Ma wasn't mad at me.

But when Mrs. Burnside came over, I was sure she came to reform me. She started out talking about Webber. "Do you really think he played well, Hilda?"

"It was lovely, Mattie!" Ma said. "You may well be proud of him!"

"Did you hear any comments from the Ingeborgs?"

"Many. Many!" Ma said.

"Don't you think Webber is a living example of the reasons why we should have more culture in West Comet?"

"Oh, that I do. I do!" Mom said.

"Thank you, Hilda!" Mrs. Burnside smiled. "Now, I've got a secret! Martha Williamson knows someone who knows that important concert soprano, Margaretta Tuttle! Martha says she knows Miss Tuttle could be persuaded to come as guest singer for the next Symphonette concert!" Right there, she got around to me. "Hilda," she said, "I was wondering, this afternoon, when Eric was there beside us on his bike. . . ."

Here it comes, I thought. I started for the stairs.

"Oh, wait a minute, Eric!" Mrs. Burnside said. "It's you I was wondering about. Are you neglecting your social life? I do hope you're planning on attending that lovely party your class is having!"

I choked. I hadn't expected this. It was awfully silent.

Ma was looking surprised. Jill hadn't told her about the party. Francie and Kristan were looking extremely interested—and I knew they would pull together on this one.

Everybody was staring at me, and Jill was the only one who knew she was looking at a guy whose party shoes were in hock at Mean John's.

"Excuse me, XYL's and YL's," I said. "I have a SKED!"

I sprinted up the stairs.

Today I Am a Ham

Well, I lived. And after school on Monday I was digging my posthole. A posthole digger does not dig the hole. You do not press a button and, presto, a hole! The digger is just a cousin of the shovel or the spade. It's the man who does the digging.

Pa came and watched me. "That ought to make muscle," he said.

"You bet!" I said. Chug! Chug!

"Here." Pa threw down his gear. "Let me take over a while."

"I can do it, Dad!"

"I said *give!*"

I watched him. Chug-chug-chug! That guy sure has muscles! But Ma called him to the telephone and the next one to drift out of the house was Francie.

"Eric!" she said. "Why in the world are you digging that horrible yawning gap in this yard?"

"Why," I said, "they've struck gold in China and I'm going to dig right down there and sneak it out from the other end."

She stared at me. "Oh, *be funny!*"

"Well, be dumb!" I said. "You ought to know this is to put my post in, and it will all be filled in."

"Oh!" she said. "Well, I knew it, in my mind. Eric, are you taking Betsy to the party?"

I almost dropped into that hole and died. I had known the family would be working on me, and I would have to go to the party, and my shoes were in hock, but it had never entered my head that I was supposed to take a girl. I guess I'm dumb.

"Well," she said, "are you?"

"I'm not going to the party," I said.

Right then Kris appeared. "How's it going, Eric? How deep does it have to be?"

"Deep enough to hold that antenna pole," I said. "And the pole is mighty heavy."

"That's what Webber said." She looked off, at the sky. "You can't guess what Webber asked me."

Francie said, "If it's about the party, this oddball says he isn't going!"

Kris was shocked. "Francie! You don't have to be vulgar about it!"

"Well, then," Francie said, "this philanthropist says he's not attending."

I snickered and went on digging. Chug! Chug! Chug!

Kris was thinking. "I guess you mean misanthrope," she said. "Eric, you can't stay away from your own class party! Mrs. Burnside says Betsy's going to have a green dress. You know how cute she looks in green!"

Chug! Chug! Chug! I went on digging my posthole.

"Eric," Kris demanded, "if you make Betsy wait and wait, what do you suppose Mrs. Burnside will think?"

"She knows her project of reforming me is not completed," I said.

Jill arrived, in a sweater and slacks. "Eric, let me try that! Your hands will be all blistered!"

I never thought of that. If I got blisters I wouldn't have to go to the party and I wouldn't have to tell the family that my shoes were at Mean John's.

I was feeling a little better, and then Jill said, "The party is coming up, Eric. You can't go with blistered hands."

Jill! *Butch!* The sister God sent me! I just gaped at her. In all her life this was her first traitorous remark!

Dot Speaker came along and Francie went out front to talk to her. Kris went in the house and Jill winked. "Kris is looking for a chance to clean the Princess' boudoir. If she goes off with Dot—" She smiled at me. And then that smile just vanished, and I saw that she was worried out of her skin. "Eric," she whispered, "I *know* they'll make you go to the party! So I'll go down to Mr. Spencer's and try to get your shoes. What did the pole cost?"

"He wouldn't tell me," I said.

"Well, I'll take along everything I've saved. So will Betsy."

"Look, Jill—" But I choked. I could see that she wanted me to go to the party and take Betsy, and Jill had hardly ever asked any favors of me. It was always the other way.

"I'll go count what I've got," she said. *"Please* don't blister your hands!"

So she went in the house and Charlie came along and in a minute I felt as if the whole world was ganging up on me. Because Charlie stood on one foot and then he stood on the other and then he said, "Look. Know what I'm going to do? I'm going to get a little wrist

126

corsage for Jill for the party. You know what I mean? Right here." He showed me, on his wrist. "It will be pink, to go with her dress."

"Your mother told you to!" I said.

"Well," Charlie said, "but I want to. Listen. Why don't you get one for Betsy?"

"Because I'm not taking Betsy," I said. Chug! Chug!

Charlie's mouth dropped open. "Pal, everybody thinks you're taking Betsy! Mrs. Burnside thinks it. Webber Burnside thinks it. I bet Mr. Burnside thinks it!"

"Betsy doesn't think it," I said, "because I didn't ask her." I choked. I think I turned purple. "—Yet," I said.

"You were turning purple, there," Charlie said. "Listen, Eric. It isn't so bad. All you've got to say is, 'Betsy, will you go to the party with me? I'd sure be happy.' That's all I said to Jill." He winked at me. "Betsy's the best Burnside, you know."

"I know. But—"

"Well, then! The four of us can walk over together. Jeeps, the four of us have gone lots of places! This is no different!"

"If you don't know it's different, you're dumb," I said. "Anyway, those other places I didn't have to have shiny shoes."

"Oh-Oh!" Charlie looked sober. "Mean John! I forgot! Well—" He smiled. "You can shine your—"

My shoes were past shining. Some little holes were coming in them because I had run that paper route so many times.

"You'll have to tell your dad about Mean John."

"That," I said, "is out!"

At supper Jill looked bleak. After supper, she came up to the shack. "Eric," she whispered, "Mean John wouldn't let us have the shoes. He kept insisting that we send Daddy over. I told him we couldn't. I told him the Kimberly game is coming up and Dad can't be told tragic things when a tough game is coming up, and he said he'd like to know why, and who did Andy Crane think he was, and would he break? He said a lot of mean things and Betsy was crying when we left. Eric, you know we can't tell Daddy. I'll see if I can polish up your school shoes. And, Eric, *please* ask Betsy tonight. Here she comes!"

She was bouncing up the stairs. I hauled in a good deep breath of terra firma—or anyway, it felt like that. "Say, Betsy," I said, "I'm counting on your going to the party with me. Will you?"

She was very, very surprised. "Why, Eric! That's a keen idea! I was going along with Jill and Charlie."

"Well," I began, "if you—" I got a poke in my lame back from Jill. "If you'll go with me, I'll be very happy," I said. "The four of us can walk over together."

"Oh, keen!" Betsy said again. She was blushing and looking at Jill. They were both just quivering, they were so delighted.

"Look, Betsy," I said, "would you like a little bouquet or something, to hang on your wrist?"

"Oh, Eric!" She almost died with joy. "My dress is green. Do you like green? Something white would go with it. Or—pink?"

"OK," I said. "I'll get one. I bet pink will look real keen."

She and Jill looked at each other and suddenly they clapped their hands over their mouths and turned and raced downstairs like two colts, to tell Ma.

I tuned up my set, but I didn't get many contacts. There was a lot of interference, and some of it was in my own mind. I was getting mighty jittery because I didn't have a report on my exam. I did contact Rhinie Bauer. He was waiting for a report on his test, too.

I pulled the switch early and went to bed and worried. I had a little money, but now I would need it for the corsage and the party and for hamburgers after the party. I could not pay Mean John for my shoes.

My head ached. My feet hurt. You don't work a digger with your feet, but you stand and stand until your feet ache.

Suddenly I had an inspiration.

In the morning I went downstairs in my tennis shoes. "Eric," Mom said, "you are't wearing your tennis shoes to school?"

"Yes, ma'am," I said. "My feet ache so, from digging. Maybe I can get them healed up, in my tennies."

"Oh," Ma said. "Well—"

I looked around. Jill knew. Just Jill. Kris is smart, but she didn't suspect Mean John had my shoes and her mind was on her geometry. Francie's was on something she'd lost, but she said, "Mother, make him get his hair cut."

So I wore my tennis shoes three days, and the big day came. Ma had my new white shirt all ironed and my new pants and jacket pressed and clean handkerchiefs in two pockets.

At party time Jill sure looked keen. I looked at her in that pink dress and wondered if she was soon going to be just like Francie or like Kris. I didn't think so. They are not so bad. But Jill has always been—well, she has been Butch, and I don't know what I'd do without her.

Mr. Carter, the florist, had delivered the pink wrist corsage that Charlie sent, and Kris helped Jill put it on, and Francie put a little of her best perfume behind Jill's ears and some behind her own, although she had her rollers on—except two locks she'd let go, because the rollers were under her bed.

Then they looked at me and Francie screamed. "Mother!" She pointed. "Mother! Eric's shoes!"

Kris stared. "You can't go to the party in tennis shoes!"

"Ma," I said, "I have two choices. I can go to the party in tennis shoes, or I can stay home. Which do you want me to do?"

"You'll go, and you'll wear your best shoes!" Kris said.

"Absolutely impossible," I said. "I have two choices."

"Mom," Jill said, "have your feet ever been sore? Betsy knows Eric is going in his tennies. She said she would be very proud to go with him—barefoot!"

"What more could one ask?" Mom said. "Kris, Francie, have you ever been offered—have you ever *given* such loyalty? Such devotion?"

They kind of gasped.

Charlie came in then and looked at Jill as if she was some beautiful art object that he had made. "Gee, Jill!"

he said. "Gee!" He was all dressed up and his shoes shone like mirrors. "Say!" he told me. "You look keen yourself, pal!"

"TNX," I said. "Thanks, Charlie. So do you!"

"Well," Charlie said, "let's pick up Betsy."

"The car's here," Ma said. "I'll drive you over, because of Eric's sore feet."

Confidentially, Betsy looked keen, too. And she kept smelling her pink wrist corsage and smiling at me.

The party was not bad. Not one bit bad. There was a long cover on the table where the pop and potato chips and cheese curls and things were, and when you were behind that table absolutely nobody knew if you were barefoot! Actually, nobody said a word about my tennis shoes except Miss Jones, who was seeing that we mingled the way we should.

I forgot to mention that Miss Jones was on my list of people who liked me ever since the theme on building a transmitter. She said it helped her know and understand me, and it tripled her respect for hams.

Well, she came close and whispered, "Eric, I can't tell you how proud I am of you for not letting an injured foot keep you at home. You show a fine school spirit by simply putting on tennis shoes and coming!"

So the party was fine and we had sloppy joes and cokes and ice cream, and afterward we all went to Fords' for hot dogs and hamburgers and more cokes, and we got home at half past ten.

Ma was waiting to hear about the party. I told her all about it in five minutes and grabbed some cookies and went upstairs and left Jill to tell the rest.

I didn't see Kris or Francie, but I wasn't fooled. I knew I was going to hear more about the tennis shoes Saturday morning, if Pa was gone.

He was gone, and Kris was just getting wound up when Francie gasped. "Here comes Mrs. Burnside, and does she look mad!"

"I'll handle it," Ma said.

I shook. I knew Mrs. Burnside was coming over to give up on reforming a guy who would take her daughter to a big party in tennis shoes.

She sure was nervous. She bustled in and walked around the table twice, kind of throwing her arms around and saying, "I'm speechless! I'm speechless!" Then she went in and looked at the painting Ma had started. She sat down and began to peer at it while she talked.

She was already out of breath. "Hilda Crane," she said, "I am shocked! I'm beside myself! I've never been so absolutely disappointed and dumbfounded—so—so *wounded,* in my life!"

She picked up one of Ma's brushes and began to dab. She said, "Nothing so weird—so offensive—has ever happened before! I mean, when you think a person is a complete gentleman, and you find he can be stubborn and contrary and—and all but insulting!"

The girls looked thunderstruck. Francie—even Kris—was white. I shook like a leaf.

Ma said, "Oh, it wasn't that bad. Mattie, haven't you ever had sore feet?"

Mrs. Burnside stopped painting. "Sore feet? Do you think that was it? I wonder—" She was almost crying.

133

"He simply wouldn't listen to a word! Every time he spoke he said the same thing, in effect. 'You have your privileges. I have mine! It is my privilege to be absent! To stay home! To be in *China!*'" She began to cry a little. "Hilda, we can *not* have a concert without John Spencer!"

All the Cranes heaved sighs of relief. Mine was loudest.

Mrs. Burnside glanced around at us and whispered. "This is confidential. I'm beginning to understand why the boys call him Mean John. He absolutely refuses to perform if Miss Margaretta Tuttle is invited—and consents—to be on the program!"

Well, there it was.

Nobody even noticed when I went out to work on my posthole.

The posthole was not a bad thing. It's pretty hard to worry about anything, when you are digging a posthole.

Bill Adkins and Don Bishop came along. "Any mail?" Don asked.

"The mail didn't come yet." Chug! Chug!

"Let me dig a while," Bill said. So I put on my sweat shirt and rested.

Don dug a while, too. "Boy, you're going to have some antenna!"

When he got to gasping, I said, "I'll take over." I looked in the hole. "TNX! I think I can see some of that gold in China!"

They laughed. "See you, pal!"

They went off in the direction of the post office. Mike

Miller and Hank Thomas came along. "Any mail?"

"Not yet," I said.

They both dug a while. When they went off toward the post office, I went on digging. Chug! Chug! Chug!

When I rested, I could hear the radio in the house. Dad was playing Marshton and the market had been down all week. Marshton and West Comet were tied. The conference title depended on this game.

So Ma would be scrubbing the back hall. I could hear the vacuum sweeper. That was Kris. Jill and Betsy were at Betsy's. I supposed Webber was committing a sonata. Francie had a whole career waiting for her in the kitchen sink. I was pretty sure my breakfast cereal bowl was the same one I had yesterday. I didn't blame the Princess. She was jumpy as a cat because of the game.

"Jeeps!" I thought. "The tension couldn't be higher!"

A truck stopped in front of Burnsides'. I guessed Mrs. Burnside got a new TV to watch cultural programs and I would get blamed if she got interference.

It was almost noon when Webber came over, excited. "Eric! Did you see what I got?"

"A new TV?" Chug! Chug!

"Nope," Webber said. "Boy, you won't believe it, but my uncle sent me the ham radio outfit I told you about!"

I stopped chugging. "You're kidding! Your uncle wouldn't waste— You're kidding!"

"Straight goods!" Webber said. "The whole outfit is up in my room! Receiver, transmitter, everything! And is it keen! Come on, and see it!"

I was going, but right then something happened. A car came along, and I heard some honks. I was getting pretty alert to code, and this car was honking in code: W9JEF W9JEF W9JEF DE W9JDG W9JDG W9JDG.

"Charlie!" I yelled. "He passed the exam! Those are his call letters, without the N! And mine! Excuse me, Webber! Our mail must have come!"

I left Webber standing there and ran like a deer to the mailbox. It was there—my license. My heart beat like a trip-hammer. My fingers shook as I opened the envelope.

Right at the moment there was not one cloud in my sky. There were big rolling pink ones around my feet and I walked on them into the house and looked at my mom and, believe it or not, I almost bawled, I was so happy.

"Ma," I said, "Ma, look at me! *Today I am a ham!*"

This was the real thing. I was no novice! Gone forever was the N from my call letters! I felt like going up on the roof and shouting for all West Comet to hear. *"Look at me! Today I am a ham!"*

Ma was happy, and she did cry and laugh together the way she does when she's happiest. "I'll make a cake!" she said. "We'll get ice cream!"

Then I heard somebody sob and I turned around and there were Jill and Betsy with their arms around each other, crying like babies, because they were so glad.

Francie and Kris appeared, and I was so afraid they were going to kiss me that I would have died, if I hadn't been so happy.

I didn't know Francie and Kris would be so glad.

They kept telling and telling me how glad they were, and I guessed at the moment everybody was on my list of people who liked me, and everybody was on my list of people I liked.

Tomorrow there would be the bedspread and more QSL cards and my shoes and all my problems, but right now nothing could make me unhappy.

"I can't listen to the game," I said after lunch. "I have to collect my route. And the paper's coming out early. I'll peddle it and be home in time to tell Dad. Or—*Ma!* You want to tell him? *You* tell him, Ma!"

I chucked the license in her hands and ran out to get my bike.

The Battle of the Antenna

I went around past the post office and told Mr. Kirby. He heaved a big sigh. "You're the last one, Eric! Every one of the fellows has been in to tell me he passed! You're all to come over to my shack tonight for a celebration. Mother's making pizzas. Isn't this one great day?"

"It is one great day!" I said.

Even my bike knew and didn't act up.

As I made collections and peddled papers, I thought of the guys. I knew why Charlie hadn't stopped. He was with his dad and had to go right on to his job at the drugstore. Besides, he wasn't sure I passed. All the fellows had been busting out with news, but they wanted to wait, too, to be sure I passed.

Later my bike did give out, of course, and of course I was at the far end of my route so I had to walk it home. I didn't dally. Because Dad would be getting the good news about my exam and I hoped he would be proud of me.

He was at home. The car was there. I burst in yelling, "Where's Dad?" Three female faces looked at me, and if the kitchen had tumbled down around my head it wouldn't have hit me harder.

"The game?" I squeaked. "He—he didn't—"

"Marshton won," Mom said. She was at the stove.

She had on her blue dress and some nice perfume. "There will be other football games," she said. "Other titles. Now wash up, because we're having Swiss steak."

"You bet!" It was Dad, in the kitchen doorway. He came and hugged me. "Congratulations, Skipper!"

"Jeeps, Dad," I said. "I'm—I'm sorry about the title!"

"Well, your old man isn't through!" He winked. "We'll have a powerhouse next year. Marshton has one this year."

At supper I knew Francie had been crying. Kris was quiet. Subdued. I guess that's the word.

But supper was good and Pa was holding up, and when Ma brought the cake he said, "We have something to celebrate anyway, haven't we? Francie, you'd better give old Harve a piece of this tonight. The guy played his heart out. All the boys did."

That was what the *Clarion* said Monday. There were no cracks about the melancholy coach. They called him a fighter. They called the team gallant.

Coach Andy Crane said, "I was proud of every one of them. Don't believe everything you saw on the scoreboard. Every man of them was a champion today!"

I felt proud and sad. It was something wonderful Dad would never have a chance to say about me.

I got ready to go to Mr. Kirby's. At half past seven I heard my call letters being beeped out front. Charlie's dad was driving us and I was glad, with my bike O.O.O. and my school shoes beat.

It was a great evening, of course. Every minute it was in the back of my mind how Dad had lost the title, but a coach's kid is used to things like that. Mr. Kirby kept us so busy I couldn't worry.

He connected the antenna to the battery-operated transceiver. He did that, sometimes, for us. "You fellows ought to know about this," he'd say.

We had always used code before. This night we transmitted by voice. Charlie was first to call. "CQ CQ CQ This is W9FWO calling any 40 meter phone, local or DX." DX is distance.

Charlie had beginner's luck. In no time he was telling a ham in Indiana, "This is W9FWO with W9JDG at the mike. The handle here is Charlie. Do you read me, old man?"

I was next. I made a contact. Mine was K9BBT, Rhinie Bauer, in Meverden, again. He was using the battery-operated set, too. This was the first time we had communicated by voice. Rhinie had passed, too!

I told him, "A bunch of us got our tickets today, and we're celebrating. Over."

Rhinie congratulated me, but we didn't make it long. The pizzas smelled better and better.

Every guy made a contact. "Remember, you fellows may use this outfit any time," Mr. Kirby told us, while we were eating. "When you're old enough to have cars, you'll want mobiles."

We could hardly wait. The older hams had mobile stations in their cars and had their call letters on their license plates. So did Mr. Kirby. Also, the older hams belonged to "Mike and Key," a fine club. Mr. Kirby said we could join now.

Going home Charlie said, "I'm going to work all states."

That would mean lots of distance calling. DX-ing. "So am I," I said. "When I get my antenna up, I mean."

In bed I remembered Webber. It was too late to go over. His mother would wonder what got into me.

I went the next evening. The rig Webber's uncle sent him was sure keen, maybe as good as Mr. Kirby's. Webber had it in his room.

"I got surprised," he said. "I wrote my uncle about your rig, but I swear I didn't do any hinting. I didn't even know Uncle Otis didn't want this outfit any more! So—" He grinned. "Here I am! Want to try it?"

"Not tonight," I said. "I never worked a rig like this. Mr. Kirby would like to see it, I bet."

"You think so?" Webber was tickled. "I'll ask him over. We'll make a few contacts. Say! How do you get those QSL cards?"

"Why," I said, "you have them printed at the *Clarion*. But you have to get your call letters from the FCC, when you get your license. And first—"

That was as far as I got. Right there Mrs. Burnside came to the door looking very happy. "Aren't you surprised, Eric? Did you dream Webber would be a ham so soon?"

I gulped and swallowed. "I—sure didn't, Mrs. Burnside!" I said.

And I meant it!

Just then I heard beeps—my call letters. We were all going to "Mike and Key" for the first time, so I got away.

The fellows were waiting in Mark Bickford's car. Mark is over sixteen.

"I was at Webber's," I said.

Don Bishop laughed. "I ran up and saw the rig his uncle gave him. What an oufit to waste on Webber! Do you know, that guy thinks he's a ham?"

"Not only that," I said. "His mother thinks he's a ham! I was just going to wise Webber up, when she came, looking as if he was President!"

"Someone will have to tell them," Charlie said. "Webber will start bootlegging around on that outfit and land in jail!"

It wasn't funny, I guess, but there were a few snickers in the car.

Mike and Key was great. We heard what hams were doing all over the country—things like relaying messages to servicemen's families and financing a seeing eye dog's operation. It sure made us proud to be hams!

Also, we heard a lot about the Chicago convention, coming up. Mr. Kirby said we were eligible to attend. "You're hams," he told us. "That's all it takes!"

Plus extra cash, I thought. And shoes.

Well, I was too busy to worry. I had to get better transmitting. I could make good contacts, but I could hear better than I could be heard. Every ham I contacted had suggestions. I told them all, "I'm getting a better antenna. Hope to work you again."

The fellows helped me. The antenna went up, and when Christmas and the birthdays were over I started DX-ing in earnest.

But Mrs. Burnside had another complaint, and she told me when she came over to work on Ma's painting. There was to be an art show, and she was determined

Ma would have something to show at the exhibit.

"Eric," she said, "I don't want to bother your mother, but I wonder if you can't stop the boys from honking for you. Is it necessary? Why in the world do they do it?"

"Why," I said, "that's how I know it's a ham out there."

So she spoke to Pa about it. I heard her, from the back hall. "Andy, those honks for Eric are driving me mad. Webber's a ham, and you don't hear rackets like that in front of our house."

I couldn't hear what Dad said, but he came in the kitchen looking worried. "Mattie seems to think Eric's a neighborhood nuisance," he said. "Better talk to him."

"I'll talk," Mom said. "I'll take care of it."

Pa smiled. And a smile from Pa was rare right then. The basketball season was in full swing and the team had not lost. Sometimes there's a little more relaxation after one loss.

Kris was setting the table. She was mad at me. I could tell. It made me feel like bugging her. "Where's Butch?" I asked her.

She knew I meant Jill. "At the butcher shop," she said. "Naturally, you mean the butcher, although you *could* call him Mr. Hinkman."

I hustled upstairs and picked up some of Francie's underwear and dropped it, whatever it was, down the chute. I hate to have the hams tripping over her underwear.

Sisters!

The next day kind of stands out for being tense. The

143

market was down. The Almeda game was coming up. Almeda had lost two games.

The *Clarion* sounded off. *Beat the drums! Sound the taps! Prepare ye! Prepare ye! Expect the worst! "We'll try! Oh, we'll try!" wailed the weeping coach. He borrowed our handkerchief, mopped his eyes and his boot toes, as he stood there in his pool of tears. "Never forget we went down fighting!" This reporter watched the terrific Comets cavorting before the tortured basket and said solemnly, "We'll never forget," and borrowed back the handkerchief, and blew his nose. . . .*

Pa is always most tragic when he should be surest of winning.

At home Sidney Temple had been over to try out a new song on Francie—one he composed for her. So Pa was letting Harve drop in after supper. Drop in. He had to stay under the Crane roof, so he wouldn't wander away and forget the time and lose his glass slipper.

Francie was frantic as if it was her first date. "My skirt-saver! Have you seen my skirt-saver?" She asked Ma a dozen times. The house was turned upside down, looking for her skirt-saver, whatever it was.

After supper Charlie came over and we warmed up the transmitter. He was ahead of me, working all states. We had a little contest going. We were having the same trouble Mr. Kirby had had—Arizona.

We sat there calling. "CQ CQ CQ W9JEF calling any station in Arizona . . . ."

No luck, but when it was time to pull switches and

leave for Mr. Kirby's, something came to me. We met Jill on the stairs.

"Jill," I said, "what's a skirt-saver?"

"Why," she said, "it's a slippery slip. Taffeta. You wear it under a knitted skirt to keep it from getting baggy in the seat. Why?"

"You live and learn!" I said. "Bet I got something!"

I ran on downstairs with Charlie behind me. We skidded to a stop in the living room doorway. Francie was sitting there with Harve. They both looked startled.

"Hey, Francie!" I said. "The mystery is solved! I found some of your underwear on the hall floor and put it down the chute and—"

She was gasping. "Eric Crane, just what does this mean?"

"Well," I said, "I thought you lost it on your way to the chute. It must have been your skirt-saver!"

She looked dumbstruck.

"Well, *you* know!" I said. "To wear under your knit skirts to keep them from getting baggy in the seat— Jeeps, you looked for it all day! I thought it was something in a bottle—soap, maybe. But I just remembered that I picked up this piece of underwear—"

"Thank you," Francie said. *"Thank* you very much!"

Charlie pulled on my sleeve. "Come on!"

"CUL!" I yelled.

"And when you see the YL, you'll get blasted!" Charlie said, when we got outside. "Stupe, couldn't you see you were getting the princess treatment? Boy, Francie was mad at you!"

"Why?" I said.

"Why, for busting in like that! Harve was just going to kiss her! Jeeps, you *stupe!* You see it on TV all the time! Couldn't you *see* she kept getting madder?"

"Well, you do a favor and you get the princess treatment," I said. "I'm used to it."

But it was never like this. Francie brought a headache to breakfast and did she sound off! And Charlie was wrong about the reason.

"That unspeakable boy!" she kept saying. "That utterly unspeakable boy! He came right to the door, and moreover he brought Charlie Korth to witness my extreme disconcert and tell everybody! And he began to talk about my *underwear!* Right before Harve, he alluded to my *underwear!* It was absolutely the utmost hyperbole!"

Mom choked on her coffee.

"You all right, Mom?" I asked.

She choked a little more. "All—all right. Mystified, though. Eric, what in the world did you have to say about Francie's underwear?"

"There you go, using the same coarse word!" Francie shrieked.

"Mom," Jill said, "Francie looked for her skirt-saver all day yesterday. Eric remembered finding it on the floor and throwing it down the chute. So he very thoughtfully—"

"So he barged right into the living room and talked about my underwear—before Harve!" Francie howled.

"I don't get it!" I said. "I thought I was doing her a favor!"

Kris spoke up. "It was the word. You should have said lingerie."

"Oh!" I said. "Well, I speak English. And maybe I'm sick of picking up her langery. Maybe the hams are sick of getting their feet caught in it, if they go upstairs!"

"Excuse me, Mother," Francie said. "I shall presume to go to school—without breakfast."

She started upstairs. Kris grabbed up her plate with some sausages and muffins on it and went behind her, and I could hear her saying, "—and 'utmost hyperbole' hasn't a thing to do with the case at hand. And the word 'presume'—"

Before I went to school I took a look at myself in the hall mirror. Digging the posthole, or something, had changed me some. I was getting more rugged. More like Dad. I had a crew cut. And my jaw was beginning to jut a little. And harden.

But I was a mess. I had a mighty short list of people who liked me. Because of Mrs. Burnside and the beeping, Kris was off the list. Francie was off. Dad didn't know I was alive.

I had Jill and Ma. And Charlie and the hams. "And Betsy," Jill said.

Dad won his game but the Anston game was coming up. The *Clarion* said, *Deep sobbing cello tones are replaced by something as taut as a violin's E string tuned up to high C. If you have an annoying remark to make, don't make it within earshot of Coach Andy Crane. . . .*

Mrs. Burnside chose that night to corral Coach Andy Crane in our backyard and complain about my antenna.

148

"What did you tell her?" Mom asked.

Kris stood there, holding her breath.

"I—got a little mad," Dad said. "You can ask Mattie what I told her." He made for the den.

"You've done it, Eric Crane!" Kris told me. "Webber will never darken our door again! And don't forget, Mr. Burnside is on the school board and the school board hires Daddy!"

Kris waited until morning, when Dad was gone, and then she came out with it. "Mother, do you know that Eric Crane *sold his bedspread?*"

Boy! The silence was like a clap of thunder. I wondered what would happen. I held my breath.

I looked around. The funny thing was, everyone was staring at Kris, not at me. Francie was mad at me, but even Francie was shocked that Kris would tell.

I said, "Ma, I didn't need it, and I needed the eight dollars!"

"You're a fine sister, Kris Crane!" Jill said. Her voice broke. "You're a sweet, loyal, loving, understanding sister! My congratulations!"

Francie whispered, "Eight dollars! Somebody got a nice bargain!"

"And she knew it," Mother smiled. "She brought the spread right to me, and I gave her eight dollars back. It was Mrs. Bonner."

I sighed, from my toes.

Frances blushed. Kris tried to run upstairs. She was so ashamed that I felt sorry for her. Kris almost never makes a mistake, but when she does make one it's a dilly.

"Kris, come back here!" Mother called. "I think I'll have a word with the lady who's really to blame for all this, and here she comes!"

In sailed Mrs. Burnside, talking. "Hilda! I hope I haven't strained our relations! I spoke to Andy about Eric's antenna. I'm afraid I overstepped. I'll never tell you—or *anyone*—what that man said to me!"

She paced the kitchen three times, then went in and looked at the painting and came back. "But," she said, "as I told him, Webber's a ham, and Webber doesn't have people beeping horns at him. And he doesn't have a monstrosity in the yard, with wires strung all over it!"

She went back to the painting.

"Mattie," Ma said, very gently, "put down that brush. Because you won't like what you paint. Anyway, you've sent Martha Williamson and Bessie Bishop and Anne Korth and they've all worked on that painting, and Catherine Adkins wants her turn next. Mattie, I feel it's time somebody told you Webber is not a ham!"

"Not a ham!" Mrs. Burnside choked. "The very idea! Eric's set is put together from junk heaps! Webber goes on the air with the best equipment money can buy! My own brother Otis—"

"Otis is a ham," Mom said. "But expensive equipment didn't make him one. True, Eric had to put his rig together bit by scrounged and traded and mortgaged bit, but he also studied. For months! He passed two examinations! If Webber goes on the air, he'll get into trouble!"

"Trouble!" Mrs. Burnside gasped. "I'd like to know who says so!"

"The Federal Communications Commission says so," Ma said. "Webber must be licensed. To be licensed, he must pass the same examinations Eric passed. And until he does, he is not a ham. Have a cup of coffee, Mattie."

Mrs. Burnside got up, looking dazed. She tottered to the kitchen and sat down at the table and Mom brought the coffee.

She sipped it. "Hilda," she said, "I can't help it! I'm all upset! I'm just so—so furious at John Spencer! I went over again. I showed him a lovely letter that Margaretta Tuttle's agent sent, letting us know Miss Tuttle's open dates. But—after all the money I've paid John Spencer for Webber's lessons, he's still stubborn! If we call a guest artist, he will *not play the spring concert!*" Mrs. Burnside wept.

Ma looked around at us and heard four "Excuse me's."

We had to get to school.

W9JEF at the Mike

Kris was definitely off my list of people who liked me and Francie was still mad.

I had other troubles. There was school. There was the paper route. I was so in debt that I couldn't get my shoes. The bike was wrecked. I was running miles in my tennis shoes. One had a hole in it.

Sometimes it seemed I ran from morning to night. But Charlie was getting contacts in state after state and I was keeping up with him. My shack was slowly being papered with QSL cards.

I hardly saw Dad. The day I contacted a ham in Hawaii Dad read about it in the *Clarion* and came up to see me.

"Time we got acquainted again, Skipper!"

"Well," I said, "I read the paper, too, as well as peddle it. I know you're going into the regional unbeaten!"

He said quietly, "It's got to be state this year, Eric."

At a time like that you don't tell your dad your shoes are in hock and your tennies are wearing out and you need twenty dollars to go to a convention. Anyway, he had to be somewhere in ten minutes.

I went to carry my route. Webber was lurking under the hickory tree. "Eric, know what?" he said. "I'm getting a shack!"

"No kidding!" I yelled, hurrying along.

"In the attic!" he shouted. "They're fixing it up with plasterboard!"

"Keen!" I called back. "Got to run, Webber!"

I knew what he wanted. I could feel it in my bones. He had his mother mad at me, and Kris mad at me, and now he wanted to ask me to help him with code. Well, I wasn't in the mood.

In fact, I was in just the right mood to do something inhuman!

When I came home I found Jill big-eyed and scared. "Francie just fainted!" she said.

There was the Princess on the sofa, looking like Sleeping Beauty, in the rose shirttail.

Ma was at an Ingeborg meeting. They were trying to work out two problems—Mean John and the Mayhew house.

I peeked in the kitchen. Sure enough, the dishes were sky-high.

Suddenly I was mad. Ever since the underwear episode I'd been getting the princess treatment. We all got it. We all put up with it. I had cleaned the basement and garage and Jill and I had done the walks. Kris had swept and dusted and Mom had cooked and baked and finished a big ironing. Dad had had a hard week. Francie had only one job, and she was trying to faint out of it.

I said, very gently, "I'll get a drink of water."

I ran and got a little plastic sheet Ma uses to wrap sprinkled ironing. I got the drink, too—ice water.

"Let's move her a little and get her head down," I said.

I got Francie's head on the plastic sheet and let her have the drink right in her royal face.

She yelled like a steam engine and sat up with her eyes and mouth wide open. "You—igorot!" she yelled. "What do you think you're doing?"

"Why, bringing you out of your faint," I said. "Princess, the dishes await without. Without help from Kris or Jill, that is. Time *is!*"

"I'll *get* you!" She made for me. Then she stopped and looked at me kind of funny. Suddenly she wheeled in her barefoot tracks and went to the kitchen howling.

Kris was flabbergasted. Absolutely flabbergasted. "You—never reminded me quite so much of Daddy before!" she said. "He has to be decisive. He's that way with the teams, when they need it." She looked at me as if she admired me, against her will. She was still off my list, of course.

I glanced at myself in the mirror—and wondered. I had doused my sister with ice water, and I felt ashamed and surprised and scared but chesty!

"I'll pick up that plastic sheet," I said. "I hope I didn't spill any water."

"You spilled just enough, and in the right place," Jill said. "And don't you dare apologize to Francie!"

"She'll tell on me," I said.

Jill's eyes flashed. "She'd better not!"

Suddenly Kris began to laugh. Not loud. Softly, like Mom. "I g-guess it isn't funny. But—*Oh!*"

She was laughing when I left to meet Charlie.

We both needed another box cupboard so we headed for Mean John's back door. We tossed cartons and

Mean John tossed insults. He had been cleaning and had thrown out some boxes that were real old-timers. Charlie got hold of two that were jammed together.

"Help me pull 'em apart," he said.

We yanked, and pulled our fingernails half off, until we got the cartons apart. That was when we found the letter, addressed to Mr. John Spencer. The envelope was old and yellow.

"Six years old!" I whispered. "It's never been opened!"

"It's postmarked New York," Charlie said. "We don't dare take it to him! He's in a lethal mood. He'd think we read it. Or that we had kept it."

"He'd think something," I agreed. "We'll take it to Mr. Kirby."

"Dodge!" Charlie said. "Here come the boxes!"

We took the boxes to my backyard. Webber saw us and yelled, "You getting another box cupboard, Eric?"

"Ya!" I made my getaway. "I'm avoiding that guy," I told Charlie. "Any day, he's going to spring at me and ask me to drill him on code."

We hurried over to the post office. For a wonder, Mr. Kirby was alone. He looked a long time at the letter. "I remember something," he said, half to himself. "Eddie Anderley helped John out in the store for a while, when he first came here. He said John watched the mail for something, he thought, something that never came. Maybe this letter got brought in with the other mail and got brushed off a desk or counter and slipped down between the two cartons. Or into one, and someone crammed the other in, on top of it." He nodded. "I'll see that John gets it. Don't look so worried."

Charlie and I were in the store when Mean John got the letter. He gazed and gazed at it. He walked around like someone in a dream, getting our parts. He didn't charge a cent. He just said, "Run along. I'll bill you later." He didn't yell. We missed the yelling.

We got outside and Charlie's eyes stuck out. "I could see part of the letter! I could see right through the page, and read it backward! It started: *'My very Dearest* . . .' That's all I saw, but I saw it plain as the nose on my face!"

"Well," I said, "you have to look cross-eyed to see that. Look, Charlie. Not a word!"

"Not a word!" Charlie said.

I'll never forget that week! Dad came out of the regional without a scratch, but he had done that the year before. The *Clarion* had a ball, with pictures of the unbeaten West Comet Comets and dire predictions from their coach, "the greatest tragic character since . . ." well, some Greek.

The sectionals were coming up. We would have two games. In our house nobody took one unnecessary breath. Francie was never more of a lady. Not a princess—a lady. She just told Sid Temple no, when he phoned. He wanted to try out a new song on her, over the phone. She handed the phone to me and walked away. She had been treating me with great respect lately.

So I listened until Sid was through howling and I said, "Very good, Sid! It sends me!"

He gasped. "Francie! *Doll!* Your voice sounds all choked up!"

"That's partly because I'm getting a cold," I said. "And partly because I'm Eric. Francie just remembered an appointment."

"Well!" Sid said. "Well, indeed!"

"But it was good," I said. "It sent me, Sid!"

I heard a bang, and Mom laughed. "It wasn't nice!" she said.

Well, I was glad Ma could laugh. I couldn't. The cold wasn't funny. I had a raw, sore throat. I could hardly talk. The big convention was coming up Saturday.

"Any chance of your going?" Charlie asked me Thursday.

"Not a chance! Ma laid down the law last night."

The fellows were sorry. "Keep away from me," I said. "I'm contagious!"

Mr. Kirby was driving the guys to Chicago Friday evening. "We'll tell you all about the convention," Charlie said, when he phoned to say good-bye. "And we'll miss you. Don wants to talk."

"Eric," Don said, "hold the fort! You'll be the only ham in town!"

Bill Adkins spoke next. "Rhinie Bauer, over in Meverden, can't go. He's had mumps and his ma put her foot down. Rhinie's broken up about it. I contacted him last night. So you won't be alone, pal!"

"Keen!" I said. "Just keen! Nice to know Rhinie Bauer is holed up ninety miles away in Meverden! Maybe he and I can have some historic conversations! Well, live it up, old man!"

All the fellows talked, including Mr. Kirby himself. "Next year you're going, Eric!"

Well, I guessed my good shoes would be too small for me, if I ever did get them out of hock. "You fellows have a good time!" I said.

Friday was hectic around home, too, with Pa's team getting off for the sectional. It meant a bus trip to Meverden, where West Comet would meet Witt.

"They couldn't make it more inconvenient!" Francie said. "That long trip to Meverden—and back in the night—and to Marshton tomorrow night for the final game. *If* we win tonight!"

Ma said, "I hope the weather doesn't go on a rampage."

The sky did look a bit ominous, but when you're bleary-eyed with a cold, it's hard to see a bright spot, even if there is one.

As soon as the bus had left Francie began to pace the floor. She hadn't asked to go, because Dad has that feeling about a jinx. Kris didn't ask either.

I peddled my route and noticed something. Mean John's place was closed up. There was a sign on the door.

CLOSED UNTIL MONDAY

Well, he never had a vacation.

I could see my shoe box in his case, and I realized my feet were cold. I wore my tennis shoes a lot to save my school shoes.

I hustled through the route and then ran home. I never made it faster. It was going to storm.

When I got home the sky was black. Ma was trying to get supper, and Mrs. Burnside was there, taking on.

"He's left town, Hilda! He has *left town!* And I'll bet all West Comet will blame me! That's the thanks one gets for trying to bring a little culture—"

"Mrs. Burnside," I said, "if you mean Mr. Spencer, there's a sign on his door. He'll be back Monday. It's three weeks before the concert, isn't it?"

"Why—why, yes!" she said. "Well—I'll cross the bridge later. I suppose you want to eat and listen to the game, Hilda." She looked at me. "Webber's been trying to get in touch with you, for some reason."

"Mrs. Burnside," I said, "I wouldn't want to give Webber my cold."

"Heavens! I hope not!" So she left, but Betsy was there and she stayed to keep us company. Because this game was a big one! West Comet had to win it and win tomorrow night to go to state.

All through the preliminary game between Rosemont and Miles the wind moaned and wailed in the background. Then the West Comet-Witt game came on. The wind didn't matter. We weren't hearing it. We weren't breathing. We were listening to fast scoring, and we were winning!

Just before the final score the phone rang. I answered. Mrs. Burnside shrieked, "Eric! This is a squall! Anne Korth says the bridge washed out above Almeda! The road is under four feet of—"

Bam! The lights went out.

"I'll hang up," Mrs. Burnside said. "I'm afraid—"

All over town the lights were out. The wind shook

the house. The rain came in torrents. We got a battery lantern on.

"The kitchen radio is dead!" Kris reported. "We won, but just as the score was given the radio conked out. Get the transistor going!"

Francie screamed. "The transistor's dead, too!"

"It can't be!" Kris said. "Let me—there!"

"You've got Chicago," I told her. "The trouble is all nearby stations are knocked out."

"Daddy and the team will be coming over that road!" Kris wailed. "We'll have to phone Meverden!"

By now the phone was dead.

Ma was awfully quiet. She said, "If the team has to spend half tonight mired in a bus they'll lose tomorrow's game—and that's the end of our hopes for state."

"They'll start out," I said. "In Meverden they won't know that the bridge has gone out above Almeda. And they won't get the news from Chicago."

"They don't even *know* it in Chicago!" Ma said. "In Chicago they're playing music!"

"Eric," Kris said, "would your set—"

"My rig depends on electricity," I said. "There's one chance. There's Mr. Kirby's battery-powered transceiver. I never yet tried it without getting Rhinie Bauer in Meverden. Rhinie has a battery outfit, and he might be looking for a scoop on tonight's game."

Ma got a flashlight on me and saw that I had on my jacket. "Eric!" she screamed. "You're not going out!"

"CUL!" I called.

As I closed the door I heard Betsy and Jill shouting, "We'll go with you, Eric!"

But I leapt down the steps and got away. Trees and branches were down all over the town. There was just one way to travel in West Comet that night—on foot. I ran like the wind, and with it. I knew just how much time I had. I knew the team would get dressed, load their bus, and start homeward. I might be able to count on twenty-five minutes to get the news through to Dad. It all depended on Rhinie!

The wind blew me up to Mrs. Kirby's door. I pounded with a fist. My heart pounded just as loud.

She was at home! Was I ever glad to see her flashlight coming!

The door opened, blowing out in a terrible gust of wind.

"Mrs. Kirby!" I gasped. "It's Eric! May I use Mr. Kirby's battery set? It's an emergency—"

"Go right in, Eric—"

Then I was in the shack. She turned on a battery lantern, and I attached the antenna and tuned up the set and began calling.

"K9BBT K9BBT This is W9FWO with emergency traffic for Meverden. Are you there, Rhinie?"

It seemed an age. I kept imagining I heard Rhinie, because I wanted to, so much.

After five eternities, each sixty seconds long, I heard him, dim and far away. Reception was not good.

I wasn't very formal. "K9BBT, this is W9FWO with W9JEF at the mike. Rhinie! Run over to the gym and tell my dad that the bridge at Almeda is washed out and the road is impassable! Did you get that? Over."

He wasn't formal, either. "Roger!" he said. "Stand

by, Eric! I'll let you know when the message has been delivered!"

I sat there waiting, hoping, waiting. It was twenty minutes before I heard him faintly. "I got your dad, Eric. The team will stay in Meverden tonight. He'll get in touch as soon as phone service is restored. If you get phone service, tell the fellows' families. . . ."

I lost him, then, but it was all right. All right. I could draw a long breath.

Mrs. Kirby was worried about me. "You're soaked and cold, Eric. And those tennis shoes! They're sopping! Oh, I should make you change!"

"It's still pouring, Mrs. Kirby," I said. "I've never melted yet! I'll be home in a few minutes and get dried up. Oh, thank you—*so much!*"

She held her lantern as long as it gave me any light.

My mother opened our door. "Come in, you poor little drowned puppy," she said, in a funny voice.

I laughed and coughed. "I made it, Ma! I got Rhinie! Dad has the message!"

The Princess herself had run my hot bath. Then they insisted on bringing Dad's big wool bathrobe to put around me. Somebody made hot cocoa.

I stopped shivering, and after a while I got awfully sleepy.

"I've got a lot of phoning to do—when I can," I said.

"We'll take care of that," Mom told me.

Then it was morning and I was waking up in my bed, and they said I got there under my own power, but I didn't remember.

"We play Melville at Marshton tonight," Francie told

me at breakfast. "And if West Comet wins, you're famous!"

I put her on my list of people who liked me.

"You're our hero, anyway," Jill said.

West Comet did win. The town went wild. The *Clarion* screamed praises.

The team was going to the state tourney—unbeaten. Every player had a write-up. Dad's picture was in the paper at least six places.

There was another picture. Mine. Right on the sports page this time. It was the picture I had had taken at school.

The heading was: STORY OF VALIANT FEAT REVEALED!

It began: *Possibly a West Comet radio ham had as much to do with winning the crucial game as any man on the team. When Friday night's squall knocked out all other forms of communication, Eric Crane, pictured above, ran a mile in tennis shoes, in a blinding deluge, to contact a Meverden ham, Rhinehold Bauer, by battery radio, and inform him about dangerous highway conditions. Bauer in turn informed the team in time to prevent its departure by bus . . . etc.*

Francie bought twelve copies of the *Clarion*, and Ma put the clipping in my New Year Baby Book.

Webber came over to congratulate me, but I had a bad coughing spell at the top of the stairs, and his mother had told him not to stay in the house if I coughed.

I'm Quitting Hamming Forever

Of course, Dad knew what had happened before he came home. I'll never forget how he hugged me. "Wonderful, Skipper! Man, I'm glad you're a ham! You sure used your head! Know what? You saved the game for us!"

"Aw," I said, "don't believe all you see in the paper, Dad."

It was Monday evening before he had a chance to sit down with the paper. "Let me have that write-up! I saw it, but I want a chance to really read it!"

I watched him while he read. I saw the puzzled look come over his face. "What's this about the tennis shoes?"

"Oh." I looked at my feet. I had my school shoes on. "Well, I've been saving these. Because—"

"Where are your good shoes? No wonder you've got a cold! What's going on?" He was barking. "I know you don't tell me things!"

Jill spoke up. "Daddy, Eric didn't have money to buy his antenna pole, so Mr. Spencer let him have it anyway, and Eric left his new shoes there. In Mr. Spencer's case, where he locks things, real safe, that the boys— that the boys—Daddy! What's the matter? Wait Dad, Eric will—."

I never saw Dad move faster. "I'll be back with your

165

shoes," he said. "And if I've got the picture, Spencer is going to hear something!"

I shouted and got hold of him. "Dad! Dad, you don't understand! Now, look! It's one of Mean John's—I mean Mr. Spencer's great kindnesses! I wouldn't be a ham! Half the fellows wouldn't have their rigs if Mr. Spencer didn't help us! Dad, the fellows owe their *souls* to Mean John, but we've got our equipment! We're hams!"

I heard Dad take a long, quivery breath. "I'll be back with your shoes," he said. The bark was gone.

He was back in an hour. "Your shoes. You'd better wear them to school." He reached in his pocket. "Here. Get new shoes for best, and get new tennis shoes."

"Dad—you didn't make Mr. Spencer mad?"

Dad grinned. "He was mad, all right, but it's all straightened out."

Charlie told me about it. Charlie heard it. "Know what? Mean John sure let your dad have it! For not taking more interest in your hamming, not financing it, making you scrounge! He really blasted quite a few dads! I was scared to death. For some reason the bell didn't ring when I went in. Then I was scared to slip out. I hid behind the grandfather clock and almost shook to pieces. After a while they began to talk like people, and Mean John invited your dad into his living rooms to see something, and I made my getaway."

"Mean John sure is a strange man!" I grinned. "My shoes are still big enough. He had them over seven weeks!"

"That's another thing," Charlie said. "Mean John

kept saying, 'I'll never forgive you! You let me go out of town, when that kid needed his shoes! I felt like a dog, when I realized!' You know, Eric," Charlie half whispered, "if I didn't know Mean John so well, I'd think he was all but bawling!"

Well, it was OK now. All OK.

And the thing coming up was the state tourney.

The excitement was more than we could stand. Nothing in West Comet counted, except the team, and that the team was going to state!

"What are our chances, Daddy?" Francie asked in a little voice.

Dad was very quiet. "We're going to the tournament unbeaten. That's a record—for us. We have a strong team, of course. One hundred sixty-eight teams started in the subregionals. Eight are going to state. The statistics look as good for us as for any of the others. We'll play in a strange place, before the biggest crowd we've ever played before. We won't play one team that we've played earlier. But—all the teams will be in the same boat."

"Have you got the jitters, Daddy?" Jill asked him.

He shook his head. "No. The boys will do the best they can. We'll take what we get. You'll see some good games."

"See?" I yelled. *"Pa!* You don't mean—"

"I *do* mean! I want you all there!"

Francie looked teary. "Daddy, if you think I'd jinx—"

"You'd be one little jinx in all that crowd, honey. You wouldn't count."

"Oh!" Kris sighed. "I *hope* we win!"

"Well," Dad said, "whatever happens, I want you there." He turned to Mom. "The girls will want to go with the crowd. Feel like driving down?"

"I think Mattie would like to go," Ma said. "She'd be another driver. We'd take Jill and Betsy. Webber will be with the Senior High crowd."

So that was the way it was.

Our team played Ironton Thursday afternoon—and won. Two games were played that afternoon, two that evening. Four teams were still contenders.

On Friday we beat Red River.

On Saturday evening two teams were contenders for the state championship—West Comet and Jackson. The press kept referring to us as "little" West Comet. And "little" West Comet was not favored to win.

I wanted to sit with Ma that night. Jill was at her other side, then Betsy, then Mrs. Burnside.

"Chin up, Mom!" I told her. "Time *is!*"

She smiled. "That's what Daddy has said, all along."

I knew how often Dad had said, "This has to be my year!"

The game was fast and furious, neck-and-neck. If we forged ahead and felt comfortable a few seconds, Jackson caught up, or a couple of fouls scared us stiff. I heard the noise for hours, after it was over—the announcers, the cheers, the terrible yelling. I could see Dad smiling, smiling. It hurt to see him, because I knew how much this meant. If we lost, I couldn't bear to look at his face.

The last minutes came and the tension mounted. I noticed Ma's hands, locked. I saw her smile.

There were seconds left when Jackson tied the score. I was past thinking, but I knew how everybody hoped we wouldn't get overtime. Overtime causes hearts to fail.

It looked as if we'd get it, though, when a Jackson player fouled Harve Bonner. Harve stepped up to the free throw line.

"Bonner has a chance to make history!" the announcer called.

And Bonner made history. He sank one, and another, and the game was over.

Ma cried, then. So did Jill and Betsy. And Mrs. Burnside hugged the girls and kept saying, "Oh, I'm so glad! I'm so glad!"

I thought I might burst. Just burst.

Several rows back, I could see some of the hams, grinning at me from ear to ear.

This was the biggest thing West Comet had ever known—since I could remember, anyway. The high school band and the Legion band were out to meet the team when it got home. There was a parade. There were speeches. There was a banquet later. There were flowers for Mom.

The *Clarion* went wild. I had Gordy Adkins carry it for me Thursday and Friday and Saturday, but I had carried the special night edition myself.

On Monday I was having a lunch in the kitchen when Mrs. Burnside came over to talk about it. "Andy isn't home?"

"No," said Ma.

Mrs. Burnside got comfortable, with coffee. After a

while, she got around to me. "It is too bad, isn't it, that Eric isn't athletic?"

"Mattie," Mom said, "I believe Mr. Spencer just turned in your drive."

Mrs. Burnside gasped. *"That's* what I came to tell you! You won't believe this, Hilda! John Spencer came to his senses! He phoned me, this afternoon. He said he'll be very happy to perform with Symphonette the night Margaretta Tuttle is guest singer."

"What caused the change of heart?" Ma wondered.

Mrs. Burnside smiled, with a little shrug. "There's no change of heart. He's always been the sweetest man in West Comet. He just—I suppose it was a little fit of temperament. Artists have feelings we mortals can't understand."

We mortals. Ma is quite good at holding back a laugh, but she almost choked this time.

So, side by side, Symphonette preparations went on, and Dad got up to ears in track.

"Relatively speaking, track is an anticlimax," Francie said.

"Who said so?" Dad yelled.

"Why, Harve! I mean, after being state basketball champions—"

"Tell Harve his head's on crooked!" Dad said. "Nothing is relative! Everything is important in itself. If he gets any notions, I'll—"

We were right back to normal. Dad was the tragic coach, with a son who wasn't an athlete.

For me everything was only second best—DX-ing, trying to be the first guy to work all states.

Some of the fellows had someone to help now, but I was too busy. I was thinking of that as I trotted home from my *Clarion* route one day. I saw Kris overtake Webber and start walking with him.

He glimpsed me and yelled, "Trotting again!"

"Yeah!"

I was in front of Charlie's house. "What did he mean?" Charlie asked.

I laughed. "Webber? Absolutely nothing! You ought to know that! Kris probably thought it had some deep meaning. Know what?" I said suddenly. "I bet Kris is going to ask me to help Webber, and she's going to hear one loud no!"

Charlie laughed. "I've got to go in," he said. "I'm ushering at Symphonette tonight."

"Me, too! Jeeps! I almost forgot!"

I lit out for home on the dead run and passed Webber and Kris at the corner. I ran faster. I was mad at myself because I was getting a guilty feeling whenever I saw Webber Burnside.

It was a great big night. I never felt so shiny and dressed up.

"We never had a singer from New York before," Ma said.

Miss Tuttle was real, real pretty and real, real nice. She had different dresses to wear, not the same one for every song. She didn't have the same language for every song either. She could sing in Italian and French and German.

And there was Mean John in the outside chair of the violin section, wearing a black suit, and playing the way he played in his back room if nobody was inside and he thought nobody could hear.

Miss Tuttle sang three old, old songs at the end of the program. One was "Drink to Me Only with Thine Eyes" and a lot of people liked it best. Mr. Eldred Burnside and Mayor Schuster both marched up with armloads of roses and people cried.

Afterward there was a reception for the musicians and Miss Tuttle, but I am happy to say the ushers were given ice cream and cake in the basement and were sent home to study.

Instead, I contacted a ham in the Yukon.

"I'll get your picture in tonight's *Clarion*," Mr. Kirby said the next morning. "It's going to be the biggest issue since the state championship, so it's a good one to be in!"

Well, the hams noticed me.

But Pa read about the track team, which had won eight events in a meet.

The ladies read about the concert. The *Clarion* was full of pictures from the concert. Mrs. Burnside came over, and when she made sure Dad wasn't home she sat down and cried. "It was the most beautiful, the most thrilling cultural event West Comet has ever known!" she said. "Now, if we can keep it up, Hilda! You *will* get your painting done?"

"Catherine Adkins finished it," Mom said. She smiled a little. "Mattie, did you see this little story in the paper? No, this little paragraph down in the corner of page eight."

Mrs. Burnside looked and almost fainted. She *almost*

fainted, and it would have been the real thing! While Ma was hustling with some coffee for her, Francie and Kris and Jill and I got a peek at the little bit of a story.

It was headed: MISS TUTTLE, MR. SPENCER TO MARRY.

"Ma," I said, "give me some black coffee, too!"

This explained a funny thing. Charlie and I went into Mean John's store at noon, the day of the concert. The door was ajar and the bell didn't ring. A lady was talking to Mean John in his living room. We heard her say, "I'm thirty-eight, John. I never wanted to keep on so long. But—we were both so proud. And when you didn't answer my letter—"

He said, "You'd trade for these back rooms, I bet." He didn't sound mean. It didn't even sound like his voice. It was sort of gentle and teasing.

We heard the lady say, "Yes. I would."

Then Charlie whispered, "Let's get out!"

We never told.

Well, here it was, and I downed my first cup of black coffee.

Of course, the hams all congratulated me on contacting the Yukon, but the big topic at Mr. Kirby's was Mean John. We were in mourning.

Don Bishop said, "We're losing one of our best friends!"

"Why?" Mr. Kirby said.

"He'll have to go back to New York," Hank Thomas said.

Mr. Kirby smiled. "What'll you bet?"

Charlie winked at me.

Don said, "We'll have to find out."

We all meandered into Mean John's place after school the next day—Charlie and Don Bishop and Mike Miller and Bill Adkins and Hank and I.

Mean John came out of the back. "What will it be?" he asked.

Don cleared his throat. "Sir, we have to know. Who's taking over your business?" We held our breath.

"I'll be here," Mean John said. He didn't yell.

We looked at him. He said, "A man doesn't go out of business because he gets married. He knuckles down and supports his wife. And house."

"His—his house?" I said.

He smiled. "It's known as the Mayhew house. It may disappoint Mrs. Burnside."

"Oh, *man!*" I whistled. "Wait till Ma tells her!"

Well, we were glad Mr. Spencer was going to stay, but we still had a worry, and he knew it.

He looked at us, thoughtfully. Suddenly he smiled. Then, before our eyes, his smile got mean. He yelled. "Don't count on any changes! If you do, you'll get a surprise! You'll find I can heave a wooden crate as hard as ever! Now, if you want anything, say so! If not, get out, before I take the broom to you!"

We got out—with him coming right behind us to slam the door.

Boy, were we happy! We were going to keep Mean John! We were happy for ourselves and for all future West Comet hams!

"You know," Don said, "we wouldn't be hams if it weren't for people like Mean John!" There, Don punched me. "Duck, Eric! There's Webber, up at the corner."

"He ask you, yet?" Mike wondered.

"No," I said. "He knows I'm ducking. In fact, he's made three cracks lately about my running. But—" I squirmed a little. "I've been thinking. Another ham in town wouldn't be so bad. Don's right. I, for one, wouldn't be a ham if I hadn't had help from Mr. Kirby and Mr. Spencer, from Mr. Anderley and Mr. Peterman and the older hams. Even from Charlie and you other guys. Hams help each other."

I gave the walk a kick. "Two or three times I've said I want to be like Mr. Spencer or Mr. Kirby—or somebody like that. It's my turn, now. Time *is*."

Before supper I went to the telephone and dialed. "Webber?" I said. "Eric. Say, I've been wondering. How would you like a little help with code, old man? . . . Great. . . . I'll be over at seven!"

The next night Webber came to my shack and stayed until nine. Kris and Jill and Betsy came in with a lunch. We ate in my shack, and Kris was all ears while Webber talked hamming!

The next night he said, "It's my turn! How about a soda at Fords'? Eric? Kris? Jill?"

"Betsy and I are rolling each other's hair," Jill said quickly.

I guess I'm growing up. "Jeeps, Webber," I said, "Mr. England is on my neck, with exams coming up."

"Next time, then! Kristan, shall we get a soda?"

"Oh, thank you, Webber! I'd love it!"

As they left, I could almost see the pink clouds under

Kristan's feet. It was her first invitation from Webber since they used to play house and she had him looking henpecked all the time.

As they left, she glanced back at me. "CUL, Eric!"
"CUL!" I said.

Something told me Kristan was in my camp—forever!

I still had Dad to go, and I didn't have a hope.

But I wouldn't have believed anyone could ever call me a quitter. I wouldn't have believed that within two weeks I would tell my friends, "I'm quitting hamming forever!"

The Happiest Moment of My Life

The town quieted down. School went on. My DX-ing went on. Charlie and I were neck-and-neck, working all states.

Kris liked me, because of Webber's hamming—and love. And Webber was picking up code real fast. "I'm surprised at myself," I told Charlie. "Really surprised at being proud of the guy!"

Charlie laughed. "I'm proud of Gordy. He's going to have a real good fist." Charlie was helping Bill Adkins' kid brother Gordy with code, and Bill was helping a guy who's our age. All the fellows were helping someone and Mr. Kirby was overseeing us all.

Actually, life should have been quite tolerable. Every local ham I contacted knew I had contacted a ham in the Yukon and congratulated me and asked a few questions about frequency and power and signal reports. This was just keen.

But there was this one terrible thing. Every ham in the state knew I was Coach Andy Crane's son. After congratulations every man of them popped a certain question at me, in one form or another. It always meant, "Are you going to be on the team?"

When I said no, they couldn't believe it. Over and over I had to find words to explain that I didn't happen to be athletic. All those words meant I was a flop and a

178

failure and a disappointment to my dad. I always signed off in a sweat.

I was reaching the point where hamming was no fun. It sure was new to warm up the transmitter and hope I wouldn't make a contact! I wondered if I was acting different—if the family noticed it.

I looked around at dinner. Dad was thinking about track. The market was low. The fellows were in a slump after the basketball tourney.

Dad had made a few statements about Harve's head, which was on crooked again. Also, Pa had put a curfew on him, so Francie was sulky—although she was being a lady.

Ma was quiet. I thought something was bothering Ma. Also, something was bothering Kris lately. She wasn't mad at me, but something bugged her.

So it was kind of quiet and all of a sudden Pa said something strange. "Is Mattie Burnside avoiding me?"

Kris gulped. She blurted, "Daddy, you can't hope to insult the wife of the president of the school board and keep your job!"

So that was what was bugging Kris!

"Kristan!" Ma said. "That's utter nonsense! Your father has insulted no lady! Moreover, Eldred Burnside has never taken up Mattie's battles. If he had, he would have had no time to—Well, I'm talking too much. I'll just say it's all Eldred can do to keep Mattie's check-book straight!"

Pa was looking worried. "Mattie gets out of sight when I come home. If she's here and I come in the front door she hurries out the back."

We all thought about it. Jill said, "Mrs. Burnside's delighted because Miss Tuttle is going to marry Mr. Spencer and live in the Mayhew house, which will be very fine for culture in West Comet. She's sure the Spencers will help the Ingeborgs get the Mainwaring house for a Woman's Club and Art Center. She's very busy—"

"Also," Francie said, "she hasn't been over much, and she does act strange. Maybe she thinks Webber's hamming interferes with his music."

"It's not that!" Kris said. "Mr. Spencer is getting Webber into Symphonette!"

"There is—something," Ma said. "Daddy, I'm sure Mattie isn't really avoiding you. But I would like to know what you said to her about Eric's antenna that day in the yard!"

Pa looked completely baffled. "Ask her what I said."

"Mattie swears she's forgotten, but her eyes fill with tears. And it's true she finds some excuse to go right home if you're here."

"Well I assure you," Pa said, *"I* have forgotten what I said!"

Silence.

Dad's eyes settled on me. Often he looked as if he couldn't understand about me. I had really begun to look grown up. You'd think I would be athletic. I knew Dad couldn't believe I wasn't.

I was getting very self-conscious about it. I squirmed.

But suddenly Dad winked. "How are you coming with the states, Eric?"

That changed the subject. Somebody sighed.

180

"I have thirteen to go," I confessed. "I hope we don't take on any more before I get through!"

Everybody seemed glad to laugh, and I got a chance to get away. I looked at my watch. "Excuse me, Mom? I have a SKED."

I went to my shack, hoping I'd contact Rhinie Bauer, who wouldn't ask me if I was going to make the team!

No such luck! If I didn't contact an Idaho ham who had a letter-writing cousin on the Jackson team! He knew all about our state tourney and even recognized my name. Ergo—I got *the* question—from Idaho!

"I suppose you'll be on the team next year."

"I have a year to go, old man." I didn't have to tell Idaho that I was a flop and a failure!

"But that's the last straw!" I told Charlie in the morning.

Charlie laughed. "Jeeps, Eric, as long as I can remember, your dad's been crying because he is an athlete and you've cried because you're not one! You'll need a new crying towel before he does!"

"You don't know what it's like!" I said. "I'm right where I was the day Coach Durbin fired me!"

"Wrong!" Charlie said. "You're a ham now. You saved the sectional game. Otherwise West Comet couldn't even have gone to state!"

"That's history," I said.

That night I contacted a ham in Maryland and told three local hams that I was a flop as an athlete. Then, mad, I went over to drill Webber.

Charlie was there. "You know," he said, "Webber's antenna could be better! It's only on a stick outside the

181

window here. We ought to stretch it to the hickory tree."

I had some extra wire, so we took time out to fix Webber an antenna in the tree. While we worked on it, my decision crystallized.

When we were through Jill and Betsy had come up, and I took a breath of terra firma and made my speech.

"I might quit hamming."

They thought I was joking.

"I mean it!" I said. "Last week exactly three out of four hams I contacted asked if I'm going to be on the team. I can't take it!"

Webber was at his receiver, supposed to be listening and copying code. Now he took off the phones. "Who's going to help me, if you quit?" he said. "I hope to get my general class license before I go to college."

"That will take some going!" Charlie told him.

"I know it," he grinned. "I can't do it without Eric." He smiled at me. "You don't mean it, boy. You wouldn't quit!"

"You'll find out," I said. "One more week like this one, and I'm signing off and pulling switches—for good!"

Betsy began to cry. "Eric, there are different ways. You were a—a basketball hero!"

"Hero!" I said. "Get *with* it! All I did was run over to Mr. Kirby's and have very, very good luck getting Rhinie Bauer. I'd gotten him so many times that I could hardly miss!"

"Run is right," Webber said. "I've wondered just how fast you did run that night!"

I shrugged. "I had run there dozens of times before. I could be the town crier, if we needed one. I've run every street in this town!"

"I know that." Webber clicked his key three times and puckered his mouth. "You said you're not quitting for another week?"

"One more week like this one, and I quit hamming—for good!"

Webber shook his head. "Boy, I'd better dig into this code!"

"Dig a hole!" I muttered. "And tell your Ma you want my antenna!"

Afterward, I remembered Webber had a funny little smile.

News gets around. The next day two guys called up about buying some of my equipment. "I'll let you know," I said. "I'll put you on my list." Then, because I was still a ham, I said, "If I can't sell you anything I'll talk to the guys about helping you find some equipment."

Hams help each other.

Webber came over in the evening to work on code, but mostly he talked. "You can't quit, Eric. Betsy's heart would break. She keeps a list of the states you've contacted. And Jill—" He shook his head. "Jill has quite an investment—"

"I've tried to pay her back!"

"I didn't mean a financial investment," Webber said. "I meant—things you can't pay for with money."

"You don't have to tell me that! And I know I'll flunk out on my contest with Charlie."

183

"Yes." Webber smiled. "On that, Jill's torn between loyalties. You're her brother. Charlie's her—her—"

"I guess so," I said. "Also, he's my best friend. I know I'm letting him down, quitting. I'm letting down Mr. Kirby and Mr. Spencer and every guy who's helped me. But—when people as far away as Idaho begin to needle you—Webber, you've never been a coach's kid and failed him! I—can't make people understand how I feel about it!"

"Well, don't do anything hasty," Webber said. *"Please!"*

Mr. Kirby talked to me. "This athletics thing will die down. Don't sell your equipment, Eric. Promise me!"

I couldn't look at him. He's a wonderful guy. I said, "I promise."

Then he said, "I saw John Spencer unpacking some dandy wooden boxes. If any of those young hams need some wood—"

Charlie and I went over to the back door and began sorting cartons. Suddenly Mean John was right there with us, looking me up and down. And what a look! "A *quitter!*" he said. "I usually get 'em sized up right. But this time—I must be slipping!"

My face burned. "Sir, you don't understand. You don't know what it's like to have everyone think you're a flop and a failure!"

He laughed—the meanest laugh I ever heard. "That's what you think!" he said. "Of course, if someone thinks you're a flop, you have to be polite and prove he's right! I could heave this crate at you!"

"Heave two, please," Charlie said. "For your dear pupil. Namely Webber."

So we got the boxes. "And I haven't changed my mind!" I told Charlie. "This week is three days old!"

The next day Mr. England called me up to his desk in study hall. I knew what was coming. When a guy is as unhappy as I was, the grades are going to slip.

"A little message for you," he said.

I hitched. "Yes, sir?"

"Coach Durbin wants to see you in his office."

"Now?"

Mr. England nodded. "I'll excuse you. You can get caught up on your daydreaming some other time."

Coach Durbin's office is a little coop, just big enough for his desk and trophies. He was sitting there in his white sweatshirt.

He smiled. "Sit down, Eric."

I sat—and squirmed.

"Nice day," he said.

"Yes, sir. I guess so."

"I'd like to have you do a little—performing—for me."

"Sir, I'm not athletic. I guess you know."

"Oh, I didn't mean that," he said. "I'd like you to pick up a little package at the *Clarion*. Could you just skip over there?"

"Sure! I'd be glad to, sir!"

He came outside with me, just strolling. A jet was in the sky. "See him climb!" he said.

We watched a minute. Suddenly Coach said, "Get going!"

He was standing right there when I came back. He was smiling.

"Thanks, Crane!" He put the package in his pocket. "You have a study period at the same time tomorrow?"

"Yes, sir."

"Report to me. I'll have something you can do for me."

When I went in the next morning, he had a track suit laid out on his desk. "OK, boy," he said. "Into this suit and these shoes and out on the cinders!" It was an order.

So I got my introduction to the track.

"I want you to run a mile," Coach Durbin said. "Yeah. A mile. Run it your way, as if you were hurrying to Mr. Kirby's. Go!"

When I was through he seemed surprised. "You aren't winded!"

"No, sir. Mr. Durbin, that was nothing, compared to—"

"I know!" He nodded. "The paper route, and getting back to do your assignments, or to a meal, or the rig, and then a run over to a ham's house, or Kirby's, or John Spencer's. Shower!"

When I got dressed he was waiting. "Report same time, tomorrow. And—one thing, Eric! Don't tell this to a living soul! Not a living soul! If anybody asks you, you're running on your own, for kicks. I want to cook up one whale of a surprise for Andrew Crane. Know him?"

My breath caught. "Yes, sir! I know him!"

Day after day Coach Durbin worked me out. I did

what he told me. I listened to all he said, especially about planning my pace.

"You run some, every day?"

"I do, sir. Nobody thinks anything when they see me running."

One day he told me to saunter out and run with some eighth graders. "You have to learn you're not the only guy on the track. Be—casual. Make like you're on your own. Don't say anything to me."

Webber phoned me that night. "You haven't been over."

"I've been kind of tired."

He held his breath a minute. "You're—not quitting hamming?"

"No! I've just been busy! See you tomorrow night. OK?"

I *was* busy. I was using my study hour for training and studying at home. And I wanted to get on with my own DX-ing. Charlie was four states ahead.

I reported to Coach Durbin next morning. After he clocked me he slapped at my leg muscles. "You haven't told anyone? This is still three-way?"

"Three-way? Coach, I haven't told a soul! Who else knows?"

"The fellow who put me wise," Coach said. "Young Burnside."

"No! Webber?"

"Webber. He came over to the house one night. It seems he had personally clocked you several times and had an idea what you could do. I didn't believe him. He had to talk fast." Coach grinned. "We're showing off Friday after school. Your dad's coming over for a look at the ninth grade. I'm sneaking you in with them."

I shook. "Coach, I'm not a ninth—"

"I've clocked you at 4.32.2 for the mile," he said. "At 10.5 for the hundred yard dash and 25.0 on the 220. You wouldn't be fair competition for the eighth graders. So I'm slipping you in with the ninthers—just for the mile. You're a distance runner, boy. I hope to hear your dad say, 'Who *is* that guy, Number 5?' "

Friday dawned—my biggest day, or my biggest flop.

The mile was coming up when I saw Dad's car arrive. He'd been held up. But he was there now, and I was ready to run with the ninth graders, the fellows he'd get next year. Not Charlie, or any of the fellows who always said I trotted too fast for them.

I wasn't afraid. I was ahead from the start. About halfway through I was all of three seconds ahead of my planned pace. By the time Dad could get his eyes focused he'd be looking at my back.

Not that I thought of that. I thought of running and coming in first, which was what I did. The next man was three seconds behind me.

I heard cheering. I knew Betsy and Jill were with the kids, watching. And I picked out Dad's voice calling, "Pete! Who *was* that?"

I heard Coach Durbin calling back. "Name's Crane! Eric Crane! Know him?" Then he yelled at me. "Eric!"

As I trotted up I heard Coach saying, "He's not even winded! He's been training himself for two years. One more year and you're going to inherit a great distance runner, Andrew!"

Dad's eyes were on me. He put his arm around me and just grinned at me. Suddenly I realized he couldn't talk! He just couldn't talk!

He didn't have to. I had studied my dad a lot, and the thing I had dreamed of seeing in his face was there now. All there.

It was the happiest moment of my life.

Suddenly he cuffed me. "You pulled one on your old man!" His voice was husky. "You—think you're smart, don't you?"

"I—I—no, sir!"

He laughed, and hugged me—hard. "Get to the showers!" he said.

Later, he was waiting with Jill and Betsy in the car. As he drove, he kept shaking his head and smiling. Once he said softly, "Gosh! How beautiful!" We turned our corner and he asked suddenly, "Mother know?"

"I was sworn to secrecy," I said. "Pa, one guy knows. The guy who told Coach Durbin I could run—Webber!"

"*No!* Gosh, Skipper! Gosh!"

We didn't tell Ma immediately. When we got home she and Mrs. Burnside were talking in the yard. This time Mrs. Burnside didn't run. She smiled at Dad. "Andy, I was just telling Hilda, Webber's going to have an antenna like Eric's. Just like Eric's! I don't care what the neighbors say. I don't think they look bad at all!"

"Indeed they don't," Dad told her. "And they're absolutely guaranteed to keep all giraffes out of the yard!" He winked. "Right, Eric?"

I giggled. "Right, Pa!" I said.

Mrs. Burnside was staring and actually blushing. *"That's* what you told me that made me so mad! That was it, Hilda! He said that antenna and those wires were guaranteed to keep all giraffes out of the yard!" She began to laugh and cry. "I don't know why it made me feel so insulted! Well—it was—you know—John Spencer! It was when he was being so difficult, poor man! If I'd only known about Margaretta and him!"

She wiped her eyes. "I haven't a thing against hams. I—I'm devoted to Eric. And—all hams! I feel hamming is, in its way, real culture! And besides—" Her voice dropped. "Hilda, Margaretta whispered the most romantic story about a letter—lost six years, and these hams, and Mr. Kirby—"

Dad gave Ma a secret sign that meant, *Hurry up! I have something to tell you!* He edged toward the house. So did I.

Mrs. Burnside was going on. "Hilda, we wouldn't *have* Margaretta if it weren't for our hams. Of course *they* don't know—"

I could hear Francie washing dishes fast. I could smell a cake that Kristan had baked.

"Excuse me!" I called. "I have a SKED before supper!"

Webber was up in the window of my shack with Charlie. I had things to tell both of them.

With Jill and Betsy right behind me, I sprinted to the house.